"To begin the Amazing Maze, will you choose Door Number One, Door Number Two, or Door Number Three?" Quizmaster's voice took on the tone of a game-show host.

Sabrina watched as three rainbow-colored doors flew together about fifty yards away from her. Stopping, they hovered next to each other. "Which is which? They all look the same."

"That's for you to decide," Quizmaster said.

"Well, since they all look the same," Sabrina said, "maybe we should just take the one in the middle."

Quizmaster stood tall, motioning toward the center door. "The little lady has—"

"Or we could take the one on the left." Sabrina changed her mind. "I guess that would be Door Number One. Or would that be too obvious? Maybe we should go for Door Number Three. That's the last one, right? Or maybe that's too obvious."

Since Sabrina was not even giving him a chance to respond, Quizmaster looked darkly at Salem. "This is not a good start."

Sabrina, the Teenage Witch® books

#1 Sabrina, the Teenage Witch
#2 Showdown at the Mall
#3 Good Switch, Bad Switch
#4 Halloween Havoc
#5 Santa's Little Helper
#6 Ben There, Done That
#7 All You Need Is a Love Spell
#8 Salem on Trial
#9 A Dog's Life
#10 Lotsa Luck
#11 Prisoner of Cabin 13
#12 All That Glitters
#13 Go Fetch!
#14 Spying Eyes
    Sabrina Goes to Rome
#15 Harvest Moon
#16 Now You See Her, Now You Don't
#17 Eight Spells a Week
    (Super Edition)
#18 I'll Zap Manhattan
#19 Shamrock Shenanigans

#20 Age of Aquariums
#21 Prom Time
#22 Witchopoly
#23 Bridal Bedlam
#24 Scarabian Nights
#25 While the Cat's Away
#26 Fortune Cookie Fox
#27 Haunts in the House
    Sabrina Down Under
#28 Up, Up, and Away
    Sabrina's Guide to the Universe
#29 Millennium Madness
    (Super Edition)
#30 Switcheroo
#31 Mummy Dearest
#32 Reality Check
#33 Knock on Wood
#34 It's a Miserable Life!
#35 Pirate Pandemonium
#36 Wake-Up Call
#37 Witch Way Did She Go?

Available from ARCHWAY Paperbacks

Witch Way Did She Go?

Paul Ruditis

Based upon the characters in Archie Comics

And based upon the television series
Sabrina, The Teenage Witch
Created for television by Nell Scovell
Developed for television by Jonathan Schmock

AN ARCHWAY PAPERBACK
Published by POCKET BOOKS
New York   London   Toronto   Sydney   Singapore

This book is a work of fiction. Names, characters, places, and incidents are products of the author's imagination or are used fictitiously. Any resemblance to actual events or locales or persons, living or dead, is entirely coincidental.

AN ARCHWAY PAPERBACK *Original*

An Archway Paperback published by
POCKET BOOKS, a division of Simon & Schuster, Inc.
1230 Avenue of the Americas, New York, NY 10020

™/® & © Archie Comic Publications, Inc. © 2001
Viacom Productions Inc. Based upon the characters in Archie Comics.
All rights reserved.

ISBN: 0-7434-1810-7

First Archway Paperback printing June 2001

10 9 8 7 6 5 4 3 2 1

AN ARCHWAY PAPERBACK and colophon are registered trademarks of Simon & Schuster, Inc.

Printed in the U.S.A.

IL 4+

For my mom
Thanks for pointing me in the right direction

Witch Way Did She Go?

Chapter 1

"And if I take Intro to Biology as an elective . . . I'm done!"

Sabrina Spellman sat back on her bed looking over the notepad in her lap. She had finally finished choosing her schedule of classes for her next semester at Adams College.

Sabrina was now a freshman in college, living in a house on campus. She shared her room with a girl named Roxie, who was not a big fan of Sabrina's cheery disposition. Roxie finished her schedule two days before Sabrina and was currently out somewhere, probably annoying someone. Another housemate was Miles, who lived in the room next to Sabrina and Roxie and already had his class schedules worked out from now through graduation and into graduate school. Needless to say, Miles was a little obsessive. Then there was Morgan, Sabrina's Resident Ad-

1

visor. Sabrina had no idea if Morgan had picked her classes yet, but assumed that she wasn't even giving it a second thought.

"No one's going to beat this schedule," Sabrina said to herself.

"And it only took you a week to finish it," a familiar voice added.

Salem, the former warlock turned cat, bounced into her room by way of an open window. Since Sabrina had moved out of her aunts' house, Salem had been dividing his time between the two residences, usually in the hope that he would be fed twice as much. In reality, he just wound up being twice as ignored.

Sabrina would not let his customary sarcasm ruin her mood. "How often will I have the chance to pick new classes . . . to choose my future . . . to . . ."

"They're *classes,* Sabrina," the cat rudely interrupted. "It's not a whole new life path."

"Someone got up on the wrong side of the kitty bed," Sabrina added, referring to his tone. "What's with you?"

"Ever since your aunts got jobs, I've been home alone all day," he said. "Life was so much easier when they were just two old maids taking care of their niece and their cat."

With Sabrina in college, her aunts Zelda and Hilda had decided they needed some more excitement in their lives. Something to take their minds off the fact that Sabrina was no longer living with them. So Aunt Zelda got a job teaching at Sabrina's college while Aunt Hilda bought the coffeehouse where Sabrina worked.

"Maybe you should get a job, too," Sabrina suggested. "I'm sure some exterminator could use a good mouser."

Salem was offended by the mere suggestion. "I don't chase dinner. I wait for it to come to me. Preferably in a crystal bowl. . . . That's a hint."

"I guess you'll be waiting a while for that one," Sabrina said. "But enough about you. Don't you want to know what classes I'm taking next semester?"

"I'm aquiver with excitement," he said sarcastically while curling up beside her on the bed.

"I'm going to tell you anyway." She picked up the schedule to remind her of the final choices. There had been so many. "I'm taking journalism two, communications, media history, calculus, French one, and Introduction to Biology."

Salem looked up at her, yawning.

"That's it," she said. "What do you think?"

"It lacks a certain ambition usually associated with one preparing to take over the world. You should have seen my old class schedules. Introduction to Rebellions . . . Advanced Dictatorship . . . gym class . . ." he said, remembering back to a fonder time. "But for a half-witch trying to function in the Mortal Realm, it'll do."

"It better *do,*" she said. "It must be nice to be a cat. The only decision you have to make is whether to take the nap before you eat or after you eat."

"Personally, I prefer before *and* after," Salem corrected her.

"It may only be a class schedule to you," she said, working up a full head of steam. "But this schedule not only reflects on my future at Adams, but it could affect my entire life."

Salem laid his head down on his paws, preparing for another of his seemingly endless naps. "And yet, they're *still* only classes."

"That's what you say." Sabrina picked up her course catalog to show Salem how many classes she *only* had to choose from. "Between my class adviser, Miles, Aunt Zelda, and even Roxie, I had about a hundred different suggestions for which classes to take. And they all seemed to think that every class suggestion was going to have a tremendous effect on my future." She shuddered as she took another look at the pages of classes to choose from, still questioning her final picks.

Again, Salem's only response was a yawn.

"Let me show you something that didn't take me forever to choose." Sabrina got off the bed and went to her closet. She pulled out a red dress with the price tag still attached.

Salem opened one eye. "You'll be the best dressed student in class."

Sabrina held up the dress in front of her, modeling it. "It's for the sorority mixer tonight."

"Sorority?" Suddenly both his eyes were open and his nap forgotten. "That means coeds!"

"No, you're not coming," Sabrina anticipated his question as she put the dress back in the closet. She was extra careful not to wrinkle it as she still wasn't sure if she was going to wear it or try to find something else at the last minute.

"Didn't you already try the sorority thing?" he asked, trying to hide his disappointment at not coming along.

Sabrina closed the closet door so she would stop staring at the dress, wondering if it was right for her or not. "That was for an article for the school paper. This time it's a real invitation, but I'm not sure if I want to join yet."

"Do you have another week to think about it?" Salem asked, referring to how long it took her to settle on one class schedule.

"They want to know tonight," she replied. "And Morgan *really* wants me to join."

"I think you should do it, too," he said before adding softly to himself, "then we can move into the sorority house next year."

Sabrina heard him.

"I hate it when you start referring to *me* as *we,*" she said.

From her bedroom, Sabrina could hear the front door open. One of her housemates was home. Finally, someone to show her schedule to who would appreciate the work she put into it.

"Wait here," she said to Salem, who responded

by curling back into a ball and continuing his interrupted nap attempt.

Sabrina hurried into the living room to find Miles, the alien hunter/conspiracy theorist who lived in the room next to hers. He was carrying another one of his telescope devices. This one was almost as big as the dining room table it was sitting on and looked as if it was twice as heavy. Sabrina watched him as he played with the knobs and buttons. Even though she had always been a stellar science student, she couldn't even begin to guess what he was doing.

"I think telescopes work better outside," Sabrina casually suggested as she looked over his shoulder.

"Outside or inside . . . it doesn't matter," Miles said in his usual manic tone. "It's not going to work unless I can fix it."

"What's wrong?" she asked.

"If I knew, then it would be fixed," Miles said with an exasperated tone. He never was one to lack self-confidence when it came to his toys.

"While you're trying to figure that out—" Sabrina changed the subject since he never would—"I finally figured out my schedule. Would you like to be the first person to see it?" Sabrina conveniently left out the fact that she had already gone over it with her cat.

"For which semester?" he asked.

"The next one," she replied, a little annoyed by the unintentional implication of his question.

Miles stopped what he was doing and gave a look that Sabrina thought seemed rather smug. "Oh, that's right, you're doing the remedial scheduling."

Sabrina knew Miles better than to feel insulted by what he said. That was just the way he was.

"Let me see." He reached for the notepad.

"Remember, it's only my first time doing this entirely on my own," Sabrina said as she handed him the pad. "Be gentle."

Miles looked the page over in his usual manic way. Not only did his eyes dart from left to right as he read, but his entire head went along for the trip. Once his head stopped moving, he looked into the air with a contemplative stare. Sabrina assumed he was gathering his thoughts, although he looked like he was smelling the air for something . . . probably aliens.

Finally Miles came back down to Earth and looked at Sabrina. He apparently had come to a decision on what he wanted to say.

"Good job," he commented with an impressed tone in his voice.

Sabrina let out a self-satisfied little sigh. She knew that, from him, that was high praise. "I picked the right classes?"

"Well, I don't know anything about the journalism classes," Miles said, looking back over the list.

"Roxie told me to take them," Sabrina said. "I had some other choices, but she thought these were better."

"Well, she would know about that, I guess," he said. "But Professor Baxter for biology . . . the man's a genius. I have him this semester, and I've never worked so hard in my life."

"Really?" Sabrina said, her voice quivering slightly at the thought of a self-proclaimed geek like Miles having to work hard at something related to science. Mind you, Miles didn't always get the best grades in his nonscience classes, but when they ended in *'-ics,' '-istry,' or '-ology,'* he always got an A.

"And that's *after* the prep classes I took last summer."

"Prep classes?" Sabrina repeated with her voice shaking some more. If Miles was working hard in a biology class, she was doomed.

Miles barely heard her as he continued. "And I guess I underestimated you, Sabrina. Usually only seniors take advanced calculus."

"Advanced?" Sabrina was confused. "What do you mean *advanced* calculus?"

"Right here." He held out the paper to her, pointing at the class. "What did you think A-D-V stood for?"

"Adventure?" she said meekly. "Like 'learning should be fun'?"

Luckily, Miles hadn't heard her since he had moved on to one of her other choices. "But why did you choose French when more and more of the country is speaking Spanish? That's not going to help you in the long run."

"Well, I lived in France with my dad for a while, so I thought I might have a head start," she said.

"How long were you there?" he asked.

"About one week," she replied, realizing that she hadn't really learned anything more than how to properly order a croissant.

"Maybe you need to think this over a bit more." Miles handed back her schedule with a disapproving look before turning back to his telescope.

"Maybe I do," she said. Then her spirits lightened a little bit as she started back to her room. "But I do want to show you this great dress—"

Sabrina was cut off as the front door swung open and Morgan ran in loaded down with shopping bags. "Oh good, someone's here. You guys *have* to see this great dress I just got for the sorority mixer tonight."

Sabrina didn't even bother to turn back to see the dress she knew would be identical to the one that she had bought. It wasn't that Sabrina's magical powers included the ability to see from the back of her head, she just knew that her luck was bad enough that Morgan would have gotten the same dress. And she had been lying to Salem earlier, it *had* taken her almost as long to pick out that dress as it did to choose her schedule.

As she closed the door to her room, she took a peek over her shoulder and confirmed her suspicions. Morgan had pulled the exact same red dress out of one of her bags and was showing it to an uninterested Miles.

The sound of the closing door roused Salem from his nap. "Funny that you're not coming back with the same happy face you left with."

"Well, let's see." Sabrina plopped herself onto the bed, nearly knocking Salem onto the floor. "Miles basically told me that half my schedule is a bunch of classes I'd be crazy to take, and Morgan just came home with the same dress I was going to wear to the party tonight."

"Is that all?" Salem asked, readjusting himself before he slid off the edge of the bed. "Pick new classes and tell Morgan to wear something else."

"Telling Morgan not to wear something would be like telling Aunt Zelda not to be smart," she said. "You know it's impossible before you even open your mouth."

"If you can't do that," he continued on a different track, "just pick some new classes. At least you'll get something done."

"I don't have time," she said as she got up to grab her day planner from her desk. She looked over her schedule for the rest of the day. "I have to get to my next class in twenty minutes, and then I blocked the whole afternoon to weigh the pros and cons of joining a sorority. There's just too much to decide."

"Amazing that the world hasn't come to a screeching halt yet," Salem said.

"You don't understand how difficult it is," Sabrina replied. "I know Morgan wants me to join the sorority, but Roxie will probably kill me if I do. Miles and Aunt Zelda would think I'm wasting my time, but Aunt Hilda would most likely think it's a good idea . . . I think."

Sabrina let out an exasperated groan and plopped herself down on her bed again. This time the resulting bounce did throw Salem up into the air in a perfect flip, then down onto the floor. Conveniently, being a cat, he landed on his feet.

After taking a moment to amaze at the accidental acrobatic feat, Salem looked up at his desperate friend. "Is this the point where I'm supposed to suggest the magical cure-all?"

"Salem, you know I'm trying not to use magic to solve all my problems anymore," Sabrina sat up to speak with the acrobat cat that had just bounced back up on her bed. "I can't keep relying on magic. If I'm going to live on my own *as* a regular mortal college student, then I have to live *like* a regular mortal college student. I can't just go around pointing . . ."

Her voice trailed off.

Salem stared at her.

She could actually *feel* her defenses slipping away.

"Okay," she said. "What do you suggest?"

Salem's entire body perked up at the prospect of being a help, or, more specifically, at the prospect of getting a reward for being a help. "A Magic Cue Ball."

"If that's anything like the Magic Time Ball, I don't think getting stuck in the sixties again will solve my problem," she said, referring to the magical object that Salem once ate, trapping them in the decade of flower power.

"Totally different concept," Salem said, licking his lips as he recalled the tunalike taste of the Time Ball. "That sent you to the past. The Magic Cue Ball sends you to the future."

"I've seen the future before, Salem," she reminded him. "It never turns out the way I want it to."

Salem corrected her misinterpretation. "Seeing the future is very different from living the future. With the Magic Cue Ball you get to ask a question about your future, and it will show you the probable outcome."

"Sounds a little like that toy, the Magic Eight Ball," Sabrina said. "You know, the one that says 'yes,' 'no,' 'outcome unlikely,' and other stuff."

"Oh, sure, to the unenlightened maybe," Salem said with a tone of righteous indignation. "But that's just a toy. This is real. The Magic Cue Ball actually sends you to the future so you can experience it firsthand. Let's see some toy company figure out how to do that."

Salem hopped off the bed and up onto the desk beside her computer.

"Everything you need to know is right in

here." He pointed his paw toward her *Discovery of Magic* CD-ROM.

Conveniently, the Other Realm wasn't too far behind in the times. They had finally decided to offer Sabrina's magic spell book in an electronic version. Granted, it wasn't as much fun to go through as the old dusty pages, but it was so much easier to haul around than the twenty-pound book.

Sabrina loaded the CD and waited for the search window to appear. Once it did, she typed in her request and scanned down the list of options.

"There it is," she said.

Salem jabbered about all the things he claimed to have invented, but Sabrina ignored him as she read off the screen. "Magic Cue Ball . . . Formerly known as the Magic Eight Ball until an enterprising young witch stupidly sold away the rights to a Mortal Realm toy company." She stopped reading and looked accusingly at the cat beside her.

"What?" he asked in his most innocent sounding voice.

Sabrina shook her head and read the instructions.

"Take one cue ball from a pool table and chant the following spell:

> *Wouldn't it be really great*
> *To know about some future date?*

So hurry up and don't be late,
Tell it to me, Magic Cue.

"Please note the rhyme worked better with the Magic Eight Ball."

"Sounds easy enough," Sabrina said before noticing something else on the screen. "Wait . . . there seems to be some small print. This is the best part about having this on CD."

In the past, Sabrina's tendency to miss the small print in spells was legendary in the Other Realm. Now that the magic book was on the computer, it took only a moment to highlight the text and enlarge the font, which is exactly what she did.

Disclaimer: You may only ask three questions and you may not stay in the future longer than five minutes.

"Well, that's good to know," Sabrina said. "Now, where do I get a cue ball?"

"Isn't there one in the Student Union?" Salem asked.

"I can't just steal it," she said.

"Steal? Who said steal?" Salem balked. "I meant *borrow* it. Once the spell wears off, you can return it."

"Are you sure it will be safe to use on a pool table afterward?" she asked. "What if there's some magic left over?"

"Can't happen," he said. "While the magic is in use, the Magic Cue Ball glows. As soon as it runs out of magic, it stops glowing. Then it's perfectly safe to play pool with. I'd like to see one of those plastic toy Magic Eight Balls on a real pool table."

"Let it go," she said. "I guess it wouldn't do any harm to borrow the cue ball."

Sabrina gave a little point of her finger, and the cue ball appeared beside her computer. What she didn't know was that it had just disappeared from the pool table where her roommate Roxie was setting up a shot. When Roxie slid her pool stick forward with nothing to hit, she wound up shooting the stick out of her hand and nearly impaling a passing professor.

Unaware of what had occurred across campus, Sabrina picked up the cue ball and recited the chant.

The ball began to glow.

"Now what?" she asked.

"Give it a question," Salem said. "How about asking it if there's any tuna in my future?"

"I can answer that one for you," she said without looking at the ball. "Outcome highly unlikely."

"Thanks a lot," he said.

"I'll start with the easier one," she said. "Magic Cue Ball, should I join a sorority?"

As soon as she finished the question, a magic porthole opened beside her. She looked at Salem, wondering what to do.

"Step in," Salem said.

"Are you sure this thing's safe?" she asked.

"It's as safe as most time-travel devices," he said.

"That's reassuring," she said as she took a tentative step into the porthole and disappeared.

☆

Chapter 2

☆

". . . **A**nd after you're done with that, the kitchen could use a good cleaning," Morgan said.

Sabrina stared at her R.A., speechless. She couldn't figure out why Morgan was giving her household chores to do and why they weren't in their own household. Quickly putting two and two together, she realized that the Magic Cue Ball had sent her to a future where she was pledging the Mu Pi Sorority. Morgan was one of the senior members of the sorority. Obviously Sabrina had been plunked down right in the middle of Morgan giving her some kind of instructions.

"Helllooooo," Morgan said, softly knocking on Sabrina's forehead. "Is anybody home?"

"I'm sorry, Morgan, I kind of zoned out for a minute," Sabrina said, looking around the room to determine her surroundings. "Can you repeat that?"

Sabrina now recognized the room in which they were standing. It was the living room of the Mu Pi sorority house. The last time she was there, she and Roxie were trying to expose a story on the evils of sorority life. At the time Sabrina never thought she could see herself as an actual member and never really expected to be back in that house.

"The first rule of pledging is pay attention, Sabrina," Morgan said. "Which part do you need me to repeat?"

"All of it," Sabrina timidly replied. "Just act like I came in somewhere in the middle."

"Sabrina, I have to tell you that the sisters of Mu Pi weren't too keen on letting you pledge again, after the last time," Morgan said.

"But I didn't have anything to do with the newspaper running the story about the cheating scandal," Sabrina said in her defense.

This was technically true. While Sabrina did convince her fellow pledges that it was wrong to do the seniors' homework when she pretended to pledge the sorority, she really had nothing to do with the newspaper article that ran. She had spent so much time debating with herself whether or not it would be fair to write the story for the school newspaper that she and Roxie were scooped by an article that ran in *The Boston Herald*. Since they blew their chance at doing an article about the sorority, Sabrina and Roxie never bothered to go back.

While remembering her past experience with the sorority and the article, Sabrina realized that her difficulty with making decisions seemed to triple when she had entered college. She had always had problems figuring out what to do when she was in high school, but somehow, life just seemed to get more difficult lately.

"Please, Sabrina." Morgan's voice took on a hushed tone that brought Sabrina back into the present. "We call it a Homework Help Program, *not* a Cheating Scandal."

"Sorry."

"The point is," Morgan continued, "we don't like to be rejected. Very few students get an opportunity to change their minds once they decide *not* to pledge Mu Pi. In fact, the only reason you're even under consideration is that I am sponsoring you. Let me assure you, they will not give you another opportunity."

"I understand," Sabrina said, properly chastised. "So, what is it you want me to do?"

Morgan gave her an exasperated look since she had already given the instructions once before. "Go to the library and take out some children's books for our charity day of reading at the local elementary school. While you're out we also need you to stop by the store to pick up sponges, soap, and buckets for the car-wash fund-raising drive. Then if you could pick up my dry cleaning on your way back, it would be ever so helpful. And when you do get back, the kitchen could use a good cleaning before tonight's meeting. You'll find supplies in the hall closet."

"There's a meeting tonight?" Sabrina asked.

"Sabrina, what's the first rule?" Morgan asked by way of a response.

"Pay attention," she said. "But when am I going to have time to do my homework?"

"The meeting should be over by midnight," Morgan said. "You can do it then. Remember, all members of the sorority must maintain a minimum three-point-five grade-point average. That's the only way the school lets us stay open since the little Homework Help Program problem last semester." Morgan gave her a little pat on the head and left the room.

"Great," Sabrina said to no one. "I have to run around like crazy and don't even have time to do my own work. I'd better get going." Then Sabrina caught herself and looked at the nearest clock. "Wait a second. I don't have to do anything. The Magic Cue Ball will send me back in three minutes."

Sabrina sat down on the couch and contemplated her decision as she waited. If she was going to spend all semester running around on sorority duty, it wouldn't matter what classes she was taking because she wouldn't have time to go to them. Not to mention that a three-point-five grade point average would be hard enough to maintain on her own, the sorority work wouldn't exactly help. Then again, she thought of all the things they did for the community, like the school reading program. But at this point the bad far outweighed the good.

Just then the front door swung open and a group of boys from the neighboring frat house poured into the room.

"Sabrina, you're here," Charlie, the head of the frat and all-around jock, said as he saw her. "We need your help."

Sabrina jumped up from the couch as she found herself surrounded by the boys. *Not bad,* she thought.

"Sabrina?" Charlie asked when she didn't respond.

"Sorry." She snapped out of her wandering mind. "What do you need?"

"You know the big game this Friday?" Charlie asked.

"Sure." She had no idea what he was talking about but figured it was best to play along.

"We kidnapped Emerson's mascot and need a place to hide it," Charlie said. "Can we use the sorority house?"

Emerson was the college that her friend Josh went to. While it was tempting to be in on the joke, Sabrina knew that Josh would be mad at her if he found out that she was involved. Of course, by the time Josh found out anything, Sabrina would be safely back in the past.

"Umm . . . I don't know." Sabrina wondered if

there was anyone else in the house she could ask. All she could see around her was a group of rather large, overly muscled boys. "I don't really live here yet."

"Oh, come on, Sabrina," Charlie said. "It's only a couple days, and you are part of our sister sorority."

"Well, I guess—"

"Great!" he said as he motioned to two of the guys in the back, who promptly presented Sabrina with a live goat. "Thanks. We'll come get him as soon as the game is over."

And the guys were gone as quickly as they came, leaving Sabrina alone in the living room with the goat who was chewing on a copy of *Cosmo* that was lying out on the coffee table.

Sabrina and the goat weren't alone for long. Two of the sorority sisters came through the front door at the exact same moment the magic porthole reappeared. Leaving the goat behind, Sabrina jumped through the porthole just as the screaming began.

"Welcome back," Salem said, trying to look innocent since Sabrina returned while he was riffling through her desk drawers. "Did sorority life prove to be everything you hoped it would be?"

"Not exactly." Sabrina pulled him out of the drawer and shut it behind her. She deposited him back onto the top of the desk. From previous experience she knew there was no point in yelling at him for invading her privacy. Eventually curiosity would kill, or at least hurt, this particular cat; she just hoped she be around to see him get his comeuppance.

"Do I smell goat?" Salem asked, sniffing the air.

"Never mind," Sabrina said, grabbing some perfume to spritz herself with. "Let's just say I'm having some second thoughts."

"Well, if the sorority's on a farm, I think you should maybe have some third thoughts, too."

"It looks like it could be fun," Sabrina said. "Especially with the frat house next door. But I'll hardly have any time for schoolwork, and I'll probably have to give up working on the newspaper."

"It sounds to me like you've made a decision," Salem said.

"I guess I have." But what if—oh never mind, it's decided now." Sabrina picked up the Magic Cue Ball, ready for more decisions. "So, Cue Ball, let's go two for two. What classes should I take next semester?"

The Magic Cue Ball continued to glow.

Sabrina looked around, waiting for the porthole to appear and take her to her new schedule, but it never showed.

Confused, Sabrina tried again, speaking more loudly and clearly than before. "I said, what classes should I take next semester?"

Again, nothing happened.

Sabrina gave the Magic Cue Ball a little shake, hoping to jar it back into working. When nothing shook loose, she put the ball down on her desk. "What's wrong with this thing?"

"You have to ask it 'yes or no' questions," Salem said. "It can't give you the future, just point out the right one."

"I have six classes to pick," Sabrina said. "How can I figure out which ones to take if I only have two questions left?"

"Be creative," Salem simply replied.

Sabrina took a moment to think about her dilemma. She had so many different classes to choose from. Not only were there classes in her major and the school-required classes, when she factored in her electives there were dozens of possibilities. Add to those all the ones other people kept suggesting, and the possibilities quadrupled. That had been what took her all week to decide, and she had the remnants of her various attempts scattered around her part of the room. Looking down at her discards, she came up with an idea and dived into a pile of balled-up paper on the floor.

"Can I join in?" Salem asked with excitement as he watched her bat the papers around.

"This isn't a game, Salem," she said as she looked through the pages. "I have to find the right schedule from all this trash."

"Looks like a game to me," Salem said from his perch on her desk.

"Here it is," she said, picking up a crumpled piece of paper and smoothing it out on her desk. "One of my early trial schedules. I think it's the most likely to work instead of the one Miles said was going to kill me."

Salem looked at the piles of paper on the floor beside her bed. Good thing he landed on the other side of the bed when he fell earlier. He could have been lost in all that mess for days. "How many schedules did you go through?"

"I stopped counting when I got to triple digits," she said as she held up the chosen page to the Cue Ball. Although it didn't have eyes to look at the paper, Sabrina assumed that it would get the idea. "All right, Cue-baby, is this the right schedule for me to take next semester?"

This time she had apparently asked the question correctly because the porthole did appear at last. Sabrina put down the Magic Cue Ball and entered another alternative future.

"Sabrina, I'm so pleased that you decided to sign up for my class," Aunt Zelda said as soon as her niece popped into the lecture hall.

Sabrina looked down at the paper still in her hand to remind herself which of her aunt's classes she had decided to take. "You know how I've always been interested in . . . Physics."

"And don't worry," Zelda said in a reassuring tone. "I have no intention of giving you any special treatment just because you're family. You'll have to work just as hard as the other students."

"Great," Sabrina said sarcastically. The main

reason she had chosen the class was because she figured her aunt would go easy on her.

"You should take your seat," Zelda said. "The rest of the students are coming in."

Sabrina grabbed one of the seats in the front of the room, figuring that she wouldn't be able to hide in the back from this particular teacher. She looked down at her schedule again. Her classes were spread throughout the day, and each of them was at least fifty minutes long. She wondered how she would know if the entire schedule was right for her if she could only be in the future for five minutes.

Suddenly her silent question was answered for her as Aunt Zelda began her lesson speaking so quickly that Sabrina thought her aunt was going to sprain her lips. As Sabrina looked around her, she noticed that the students were taking notes just as quickly as her aunt spoke. Then Sabrina realized that she, too, was moving at the heightened speed.

Sabrina had moved at hyperspeed before, but this time the world was moving along with her and she was having some trouble keeping up. It was a weird experience as she filled four pages of notes and got a killer homework assignment in only a matter of seconds.

Before she even had a chance to think about her first class, she was almost through her second. The journalism class she had been told to take proved to everything that she heard it would be. She wanted to take that one. Her third class was another journalism class, and looked pretty good, too. But the best thing about it was that it was followed by lunch.

Scarfing down her food, Sabrina worried about getting sick from eating so fast, but was halfway through class number five before she realized that she was getting hungry again. The last class of the day ended with seconds to spare in the five minutes. During those seconds, she decided that the final three classes were also keepers. The only questionable one was her aunt's class. Would her aunt feel hurt if she didn't take it? She put her worries aside as the porthole arrived to take her back to the past.

For the second time, Sabrina dropped to her bed. This time, not only was she overwhelmed, she was exhausted as well. She had just taken an entire day of class notes in the space of five minutes, and she had the cramp in her hand to prove it. Unfortunately, she didn't have the notes since they had to be left in the future.

"Long day?" Salem asked. He was still on the desk as she had left him before her latest trip into the future. This time he had managed to shut all the drawers he was pawing through before she got back to the room.

"I'm ready for bed," she replied, pulling her covers over her.

"And just in time for your real classes to begin," he said.

Sabrina bolted up, checking her clock. "Great,

I have two minutes to get all the way across campus."

"And yet, with a mere point of the finger you can be there in two seconds," Salem reminded her. "But first, what about your classes?"

"It looks like a pretty good schedule. Once I drop Aunt Zelda's class." Sabrina grabbed a pencil and crossed physics off the list. She would worry about choosing another class to fill the hole later.

Sabrina gathered the books for her morning classes in the present timeframe. Once she had everything, she put it all in her backpack and started for her door.

"What about your third question?" Salem asked, eyeing the Magic Cue Ball. "You still have your dress dilemma."

"Like I'm going to waste this on a dress," Sabrina said as she picked up the glowing Cue Ball. "I think I'll see what happens today and come back later with one really good question."

"Suit yourself," Salem said as he moved over to her windowsill. "In the meantime, I'll just curl up in this sunbeam and have a nap."

"You do that," Sabrina put the Cue Ball back down as she continued toward the door. "See you later."

There was no response except for Salem's snores.

As soon as Sabrina left the room, Salem's eyes half-opened while he continued his fake snoring. Once he saw that the coast was clear, he fully opened his eyes and stopped the snoring. His "nap" over, Salem made his way back to Sabrina's desk and the Magic Cue Ball.

"Well, since Sabrina's not going to be using this," he said to no one, "maybe I'll just see what my future holds."

Chapter 3

☆

☆

"**M**ore caviar for you, sire?" Hilda asked, holding a polished silver platter full of the overpriced fish eggs.

"More pâté?" asked Zelda, brandishing her own platter.

"Or would you rather have some pheasant under glass?" Sabrina added to the gourmet food-fest.

"Yes, yes, and yes!" Salem nodded to each of the platters. "But please remove the pheasant from under the glass. It's so hard for me to do it without thumbs."

"As you wish." Sabrina did as she was told, placing the cooked pheasant on a table in front of the cat.

Salem was lying on an overstuffed bed just perfect for his size. With linens of silk and satin and the most plush down pillows he could imagine, he was on his perfect throne. The bed was in the exact center of a circular room with gold and silver trim. There were several floor-to-ceiling windows so he could look out at his kingdom and two enormous double doors made entirely of gold to keep out the riffraff. It was the room he had dreamed of his entire life.

And all this just for asking if I would be happy ruling the world, he thought to himself.

Salem had used Sabrina's final question for his own selfish desires. Of course, he didn't care about that right now. All that he could concentrate on were his own needs.

The king surveyed his throne room. His entire royal court, not just the Spellman women, surrounded him.

Men were fanning him with oversize palm fronds and women tending to the filing of his claws. On the floor in front of him entertainers performed for his pleasure alone. There was even a man peeling grapes for Salem. It was everything he had ever dreamed of, except that in his dreams, he was usually human again.

"Someone," Salem said, and the whole room froze at attention. He had a silent chuckle, excited by his own power. "Someone, please fluff my pillows."

Half the people in the room nearly trampled each other to do as their ruler wished. Sabrina won out and began to fluff. Her aunts made themselves busy spooning caviar and pâté onto crackers and feeding the feline.

Salem smiled as he settled in to the plush bedding. The only part of his body that moved was his jaw as he chewed on the hand-fed snacks.

The relaxation was interrupted when Drell, the *former* head of the Witches' Council, entered Salem's chambers through the gold double doors.

Being as heavy as they were, the doors slammed upon Drell's entrance, rousing Salem out of his rest.

"Pardon me, sir," Drell said in a bow so deep that his shoulder-length hair actually touched the floor. "But there is a slight problem."

"What now?" Salem asked. Though he was bothered by the interruption, Salem did take some glee out of watching the oversize man have to get down on all fours. "Don't tell me we're having another slave revolt."

"Oh, no, no, sire. Nothing that grand," Drell said, paling at the fact that his king was upset. "Just a minor concern—a trifle, really."

"Go on," Salem said, eyeing his food. His subjects had stopped feeding him when Drell entered the room.

"It's your army," Drell said.

"What could possibly be the problem?" Salem asked. "I rule the world; there's no one for them to fight."

"That's the problem exactly, my lord," Drell said. "They're getting bored standing around with nothing to do . . . since the slave revolt, that is."

"Ah, I see," Salem said as he thought over the

problem. "As a very wise leader once said, 'Let them eat cake.' "

"But, sir," Drell said, still on his knees. "That hardly solves the problem. In fact, that has been your solution to every problem."

"Are you questioning my methods?" The cat stood on all fours, arching his back.

Everyone in the room froze upon hearing the angered tone of their leader.

Immediately Drell's head dropped to the floor, bowing in fright. "I apologize, my king. No disrespect intended."

Salem settled back down. "Very well, then. Make it so."

"Yes, Your Highness," Drell said and left the room, sliding backward on his knees, bowing all the way out the door.

"Drat," Salem said. "Sabrina?"

"Yes, my king!" She snapped to attention beside him.

"Next time he comes back, remind me to have him turn me back into a man."

"Yes, my king."

Sabrina was handed the plate of peeled grapes and was about to feed them one by one to Salem, when the magic porthole reappeared to take him back.

"Oh, no, you don't," Salem said to the porthole.

His subjects looked at him, wondering which of them he was talking to. They could not see the porthole and had no idea what was going on.

Ever ready, they listened for instructions, just in case he was addressing them.

"I have no intention of going back now," Salem continued as he backed away to the far end of his bed. He was almost teetering off the edge.

"Sire," Sabrina interrupted. "Is something wrong?"

"Nothing," he replied. "Nothing at all."

The porthole inched toward him. Salem jumped into Sabrina's arms as it got closer. Realizing that he wasn't safe, Salem dropped to the floor and began to run.

The porthole gave chase.

As the cat ran around the room each servant bowed as he approached them. It looked as if the room was suddenly full of fans at a baseball game doing the wave as, round and round, they bowed as their leader ran past them.

After three circles of the room Salem leaped into Sabrina's arms, yelling, "I need a spell to make this room a magic-free zone!"

Hoping to please their king, all the witches in the room cast the spell immediately. The combined power was enough to counteract the porthole, sending it out the door.

The porthole tried to push its way back into the room, but an invisible force field kept the porthole safely locked out.

"That's better," Salem said. "I know a good thing when I've got it. I'm not going back in five minutes. I'm not going back at all!"

The magic porthole loomed outside the open doorway, ominously stalking the cat. His five minutes of future had expired, and the porthole was determined to get him back to where—and when—he belonged.

"Someone close those doors!" Salem bellowed.

Again, his subjects fell all over each other to carry out his wishes, slamming the door on the unseen porthole.

Gone, but not forgotten.

Meanwhile, back at the campus . . .

"You have all of history to choose from," Sabrina's ultra-cool, ultra-cute young history professor said as he paced the front of the lecture hall. "One person. One historical figure who you feel was the greatest influence of your life."

Sabrina finished writing the assignment and looked up at the clock. When her eyes came back down, she noticed that she had been noticed, noticing the time.

"Yes, Miss Spellman," the professor said with a warm smile that kept the attention from being awkward. "Class dismissed."

Sabrina smiled an embarrassed little smile back as she grabbed her books and put them in her backpack. She stalled herself a little so it didn't appear that she was too eager to leave. It wasn't that she wanted to leave his class, but she did have to get to work at the coffeehouse. Aunt Hilda was still getting used to running the place, and she was a little bit of a dictator, especially when it came to reporting late for work.

"Miss Spellman, would you mind waiting a minute?" Professor Murphy said as he approached her desk.

"Sure," Sabrina said while trying not to stare into his deep brown eyes. She put down her book bag and gave him her full attention, noticing that she was the only student left in the room.

"I read your article in the school paper covering the student government elections," he said as he sat on the edge of the desk beside hers.

"You did?" she asked with a surprised tone to her voice. A new smile crept to her face knowing that not only did he read the article, but he also knew that she had written it. Actually, she *and* Roxie had written the article, but Roxie wasn't in his class, and Sabrina didn't think to bring her up.

"Of course," he said. "I oversee the student government, so I have to keep up on what the student body thinks."

"Oh," she replied, a little disappointed. It was much nicer to think he was specifically looking for her work.

"You have some really great ideas," he continued.

"Thanks," Sabrina said and realized that her entire end of the conversation had consisted of only one- or two-word responses, never going over two syllables. "I've always felt that students need to be involved in the way the school is governed. I was just doing my part."

"That's exactly why I wanted to speak with you," he said. "Now that the elections are over, we have some openings in what we refer to as the student cabinet. It's a group of students who act as advisers to the class president. I think you'd be perfect to fill one of the spots."

"Really?" Sabrina was shocked by the unexpected request. "I'd love to . . . I mean, I can't . . . I mean, I want to, but I don't know."

Professor Murphy looked confused by Sabrina's response or lack thereof. "Why don't you take some time to think about it."

"Oh . . . okay, thanks," Sabrina finished putting away her books and left the room.

Once out in the hallway she nearly ran right into her aunt Zelda.

"Careful, honey," Zelda said as she grabbed on to her niece before the collision. "Are you okay?"

"Yeah," Sabrina said, looking back into the room. "If you count making a total fool of yourself in front of one of the cutest professors in the school as being okay."

"Sabrina," Zelda said. "You shouldn't think of your professors that way."

"Aunt Zelda, he's cute. That's all," Sabrina said as she started walking down the hall. "Nothing's going to happen. This isn't one of those dramas on the WB."

"Even though you're in college, I'm still your

aunt," Zelda said as she walked with her niece. "That means I can still worry about you. Now, why do you think you made a fool of yourself?"

"He asked me if I wanted to be in student government," she said plainly.

Zelda waited for more of an explanation. It didn't come. "And you don't want to be in student government?"

"No," Sabrina said. "I mean, yes, but I don't think I should."

"Why?" Zelda prodded her for a clearer answer. She was used to this line of dialogue with her niece and was patient enough to let it run its course.

"I can't work on the school paper *and* be in student government," Sabrina said, as if that were all the answer she needed.

"Why not?" Zelda held the door open for her as they left the building and stepped out into the campus Quad.

Sabrina led them in the direction of the coffeehouse where she worked. It was one of those beautiful Westbridge days where they could walk freely without coat or umbrella. The weather would be changing soon, so they knew to enjoy a good thing while they had it.

"Don't you think it's a conflict of interest?" Sabrina asked her aunt. "To be a part of the governing body *and* a member of the media? What if something big happened at the school, and I couldn't write about it because of my position?"

"Sabrina, students do it all the time," Zelda

said. "It's not that big of a conflict while you're in school. Besides, real politicians often contribute articles to real newspapers."

"I guess," Sabrina said as she ducked to avoid being beaned by a rogue Frisbee flying across the Quad. "It's just one more thing I have to think about. He also gave us an assignment to write a paper on a historical figure. Got any suggestions?"

"There's always Leonardo da Vinci," Zelda said, taking on a gossipy tone. "Oh, the stories I could tell you about Leo."

"Thanks," Sabrina said. "But I've found it's better to rely on books for my history reports and not stories relayed to me by first-hand witnesses."

"Good point," Zelda said. "But I did have something else I wanted to talk to you about, which is why I'm so glad I ran into you."

"Better make it quick," Sabrina said. "We're almost at the coffeehouse, and you know how Aunt Hilda can be about personal discussions during work."

"Oh, that's right," Zelda said. "Well, this is about work anyway."

"What about it?" Sabrina asked.

"The school has found some additional funding for the science department," Zelda said.

"Congratulations," Sabrina replied. "But what does this have to do with me?"

"I can hire a part-time office assistant a few afternoons a week," Zelda said as they reached the coffeehouse. "I thought you might want to work with me on the afternoons you aren't here."

Sabrina froze in her tracks at the thought of another decision to make.

"You can take some time to think about it," Zelda said, sensing a possible meltdown. "I only offered so you might have some extra spending cash. And I do miss having you around since you moved out."

"No, it's not that." Sabrina snapped out of it. "I mean, thank you. I *will* think about it. I've just got a lot on my mind lately."

"It's okay, honey," Zelda said as she opened the door to the coffeehouse. "I don't need an answer until Monday."

"Thanks," Sabrina said for both the door and the short reprieve before having to make another decision.

Together they walked into the coffeehouse. Zelda veered off to say hello to her sister while Sabrina was immediately approached by her roommate Roxie.

"Well?" Roxie asked Sabrina without bothering to provide the subject of their discussion.

"Well, what?" Sabrina asked.

"Are you going to take tennis lessons with me?" Roxie looked annoyed, which was nothing new for her. "I asked you this morning. You said you'd get back to me."

"Yeah," Sabrina said.

"You will?!" Roxie showed a rare moment of

excitement before turning back to her usual stern face.

"No," Sabrina corrected her. "I meant 'Yeah, I remember,' not 'Yeah, I'm going to do it.' I still have to decide."

"What's taking so long?" Roxie asked.

"Why are you taking tennis lessons?" Sabrina asked, trying to deflect her roommate's question with a question of her own. "You're not exactly the sporting type."

"I explained this earlier," Roxie reminded her. "It's either take the extra lessons or fail gym class. Sabrina, only losers fail gym class."

"I happen to know some wonderful people who failed gym," Sabrina said.

"You would," Roxie replied. "So, are you going to take the lessons?"

"Sabrina, you're already late," Hilda said as she crossed over to her niece. "Do you really think you should be engaging in personal conversations, too?"

Sabrina had been so busy trying to figure out what to tell Roxie that she hadn't noticed that Zelda was no longer keeping Hilda busy.

"Sorry, Rox," Sabrina said, thankful for the reprieve. "I have to get to work."

"Fine," Roxie said. "But let me know soon."

Sabrina watched as her roommate left the coffeehouse, wondering how she was ever going to find the time to do all the different things people wanted her to do. *If I could only be more like*

Roxie, Sabrina thought to herself. *She never seems to have problems making decisions . . . or forcing other people to make them.*

"Sorry, Aunt Hilda," Sabrina said, with her mind back on her job. "I had to talk to my professor after class for a few minutes."

"It's okay," Hilda said. "I just had Josh work twice as hard until you got here."

Sabrina gave a compassionate glance to her overworked friend, who was in the middle of making her Aunt Zelda a cappuccino. He had the same frazzled look he always had on his face since Hilda took over the place. With his dark hair mussed and eyes slightly glazed over, he looked even cuter to Sabrina. She would never forgive herself for giving up the chance to turn their friendship into a relationship.

"I'll get right to work," Sabrina said as she started for the back room to put away her things and get her apron. "It's been a rough day."

"But first," Hilda stopped her, "I was wondering if you could pick up extra hours for the next month. Until I can hire someone for the late shift?"

Suddenly Sabrina's vision began to blur. The room seemed to be circling her as if it were moving. She felt her aunt's hands grab on to her face as her sight cleared to see Hilda with a look of concern.

"Sabrina, are you all right?" Hilda asked. "Your head was spinning."

"Don't I know it," Sabrina said. "My mind's been racing all day."

"No, I mean your head was actually *spinning.*" Hilda motioned for Zelda to come over and join them. "It happens when a witch is thinking of too many things at the same time. It's actually where the mortal cliché comes from."

"What's wrong?" Zelda asked as she joined them.

"Sabrina's head was moving faster than a twister," Hilda said. "I thought we'd have to board up the windows and tie down the cows."

"Oh, dear," Zelda said. "I was afraid of that. You need to get some rest, honey."

"But I have to work," Sabrina lamely said, although her mind was a million miles away from making other people coffee.

"You take the afternoon off," Hilda said. "Josh can handle things."

"I'll take you home," Zelda said and ushered Sabrina to the door without giving her the chance to respond.

All Sabrina could do was watch poor Josh look even more frantic as the afternoon coffee crowd made their way to the counter.

Aunt Zelda saw Sabrina safely to her front door before going home. Sabrina was a little more calm than when they had left the coffee-house, looking forward to using the Magic Cue Ball to solve at least one of her problems. She even let out a little smile as she waved goodbye to her aunt.

The smile did not last long.

As soon as Sabrina opened the front door, Miles attacked her. "Sabrina, I need to ask you—"

"No!" she screamed and covered her ears, running to her bedroom. "No more questions, no more favors. I can't take it!"

She slammed the door behind her, leaving Miles staring at the back of it. Of course, having lived with Sabrina for a while now, he was used to crazy outbursts like this.

In her bedroom Sabrina collapsed into the chair next to her desk. She picked up the glowing Cue Ball and stared into it. There was some comfort in the fact that she still had one question that could be solved.

"But which question?" she asked no one.

Sabrina put down the Cue Ball, fearing she might accidentally ask a question while it was in her hand. As she put the Cue Ball back on her desk, Sabrina noticed the bent corner of a picture sticking out of one of the drawers Salem had been rifling through earlier. She opened the drawer so that the photo wouldn't get any more damaged than it already was. Sabrina instantly regretted that action when she realized that it was a picture of Harvey. It was the last photo of him that she had since they had gone off to different schools. All of the questions nagging at her went away for a moment while she looked at his face.

She and Harvey had been dating pretty much all through high school. Sure, every now and then they had the typical difficulties that every high school couple goes through. Harvey's parents and Sabrina's aunts thought they were spending too much time with each other, and they both started seeing other people for short periods in their relationships. And, of course, her attraction to Josh certainly got in the way. But it was the *unnatural* problems, associated with Sabrina being a witch, that caused the biggest strain on their relationship.

Folding back the bent edge of the photo, Sabrina put the picture back in her desk.

Since sitting and dwelling on her past wasn't helping her with her present, Sabrina got up so she could pace while she reasoned things out loud. "Okay, the most important questions should be about work. Either I should take the job with Aunt Zelda or take on additional hours with Aunt Hilda. Of course, if I do either of those things I might not have time to join student government or take tennis lessons. So then what's more important, work or school? Not to mention that I still have to come up with a topic for my history paper."

Sabrina stopped mid-pace. If she were a cartoon character, a lightbulb would have just gone off above her head. "Be creative!"

After remembering Salem's advice from earlier, Sabrina sat back at her desk and picked up the Magic Cue Ball. "Okay, since this is my last chance, I'll just give you the mother of all questions." She took a deep breath. "Should I join student government and start taking tennis lessons while getting a second job, picking up some extra shifts at the coffeehouse, and writing about Queen Elizabeth for my history paper?"

The Magic Cue Ball glowed brighter and brighter, but no porthole formed. Slowly it changed color to an angry red as it grew hotter in Sabrina's hand. Soon the cue ball was so hot that she was forced to drop it onto the floor. As it crashed down beside her the Magic Cue Ball exploded in a flood of light.

Once Sabrina's eyes readjusted so she could see, she realized that she was no longer in her bedroom. In fact, she didn't think she was on campus or even in the Mortal Realm at all.

Sabrina was floating in space.

Luckily, Sabrina knew from past visits to Mars and the other planets that witches could breathe in the vacuum of space. It didn't get her home, but it was nice to know she wasn't going to suffocate.

As she wondered what she was doing there, Sabrina noticed, oddly enough, three rainbow doors flying around like comets. There was also a collection of paintings zooming past her. They seemed to be portraits, but Sabrina could hardly make out any of them out since they were flying by so quickly. Sabrina didn't know of any art galleries in space, and there was no one around to ask where she was. She was entirely alone except for the doors, the portraits, and the distant stars.

"Somehow," Sabrina's voice echoed through the empty space, "I don't think this is the answer I was hoping for."

Chapter 4

Salem couldn't fall asleep. He had been trying to nap for the past hour, but sleep would not come. It wasn't because of the porthole that he knew was still outside the door to his chamber. No, it was because of his very subjects. They were all trying so hard to be quiet that their continued shushing of one another only managed to irritate Salem and keep him awake.

"Shhh, the king is trying to sleep," Zelda said.

Which was met with a response from Hilda. "If you weren't shushing us, it *would* be quiet in here."

Which was naturally followed by Sabrina chiming in, "Both of you be quiet, the king is trying to sleep."

And so on, and so on, and so on . . .

It didn't matter anyway, as Salem was about to be awakened from whatever sleep he may have fallen into.

BANG!

The noise came from the double doors of his chamber. Instantly Salem perked up to see if the porthole had come in. The doors were still shut, but Salem noticed that his subjects had heard the bang, too. The porthole may have been invisible to them, but the noise it made was obviously not.

BANG!

His eyes now fully open, Salem actually saw the door buckle inward. The porthole was trying to come in, and the heavy gold doors were not going to stop it.

All of his subjects were looking to him for guidance. Instinctively they stood between their king and the threat on the other side of the door.

BANG!

"Quick!" he said. "I need a spell to keep those doors shut!"

"But, sire," Sabrina reminded him, "you had us turn this into a magic-free zone."

"Well, undo the spell!" He had to yell over the continued banging on the door as the porthole increased its attack.

"To do that, we'd need to use magic!" Sabrina yelled back, pointing out the flaw in his logic.

"Which you don't have in a magic-free zone," Salem finished her thought. "And I thought I was being so clever. Well, someone, go block the door."

At once, his subjects started for the doors. A few had reached them and were holding them back, but it was too late. The subjects were thrown to the ground as the double doors burst open in a shower of splintered gold. The porthole was now a swirling red mass on the attack.

Knowing that his subjects would be no match for the porthole they couldn't even see, Salem leaped from his bed and ran to the back of the room. The porthole would not take him without a fight.

Suddenly the fight went out of him as he saw the porthole grow to twice its original size. It was approaching him at breakneck speed. Salem reared back, but he knew there was nowhere to run. The giant porthole passed through the royal court as if they weren't even there and flew at Salem, swallowing him whole.

Sabrina was still floating through space, her hair tangled across her face.

She managed to use her arms to swing her body around so that her hair naturally flowed down her shoulders. Now she was able to see a path in the distance beyond the flying doors and portraits. Someone had built a walkway in the middle of space.

Sabrina didn't bother to wonder who put it there or why it even existed. She just pointed her finger to let her magic take her there.

Nothing happened.

She pointed again and got the same result. Nothing.

"Great." She examined her magic finger, giving it a little shake. "This thing's on the blink again."

Sabrina tried swimming through space like she was in a pool. All she managed to do was turn her body to the side. Without her magic she was stuck in the middle of space with no way to get home.

Then things went from odd to bad when Sabrina noticed that one of the floating portraits was on a collision course with her. Flailing her arms, Sabrina tried swimming through space again, but to no use. As the frame loomed closer, Sabrina managed to position herself so that she could grab the portrait when it reached her.

Gotcha! She latched on to the back of the painting hoping it would carry her to the walkway. Once she had contact with solid ground, she hoped she might be able to take the path to some kind of exit.

Sabrina climbed around so that she could see who or what she had hitched a ride on.

The first thing Sabrina noticed when she got to the front of the painting was that the woman in the portrait was wearing a really cool leather aviator jacket and was dressed in a style from the thirties. A plaque on the painting read: Amelia Earhart: Lost during her flight across the Pacific Ocean.

Sabrina had learned about Amelia Earhart back in high school. She was the first female pilot to fly over the Atlantic Ocean alone. She disappeared in 1937 when she and her co-pilot were attempting to break another record and fly around the world. Over the years since their disappearance there were many stories told about what might have happened to them. Some people even believed they had been abducted by aliens.

Pulling her attention away from the painting, Sabrina saw one of the big rainbow doors approaching about to sideswipe the Earhart portrait, or more specifically, sideswipe Sabrina right off the Earhart portrait. Sabrina glanced around frantically. Another painting was flying nearby. Sabrina leaped for it as it passed.

This time she landed on the front of the painting and found herself resting on a portrait of Christopher Columbus. His plaque credited him with getting lost on the way to Asia.

"Okay," Sabrina said out loud to no one. "Obviously we've got a theme going here."

"And where exactly is here?" a familiar voice hollered back.

"Salem?" Sabrina turned her head to see her favorite feline surfing his way toward her on another portrait.

"Incoming!" he yelled as he launched himself from his makeshift surfboard onto her portrait, nearly shredding the painting with his claws as he tried to hang on.

Sabrina grabbed him and tucked him under her arm. There was no time for pleasantries since they were approaching the path, and it was now or never. "Hold on!"

Sabrina jumped from the portrait and did a little roll as she and Salem landed on the walkway.

"Thanks . . . I think." Salem was a little shaken by the two quick jumps.

Sabrina remained seated on the ground. No telling what would happen if she tried to get up. "Where did you come from?"

"A much better place than this," he said. "What are we doing here?"

"I guess I asked the Magic Cue Ball one too many questions," she said, giving him a little rub behind the ears.

Salem blushed under his fur at the fact that he had used—and abused—the third question. "Ummm . . . about that—"

"I asked for six different futures at the same time," she continued. "I guess I overloaded it."

Relieved, Salem decided not to admit to his part. "You should know better than to break the rules of magic."

"But why did it send you here, too?" She asked.

"Where is *here,* anyway?" Salem quickly changed the subject.

"Well, I can safely say you ain't in Kansas no more," a third voice added to the vacuum of space.

Sabrina knew that voice and was up like a shot looking around. As the paintings and doors continued to fly around her, she caught a glimpse of neon-colored clothing behind them. Then, suddenly, everything parted and she saw an old friend floating above her.

"Quizmaster!" Sabrina exclaimed upon seeing the man who helped her prepare for her Witch's License. She hadn't seen him in a few years, but she remembered how it was so like him to either pop in or pop her out of someplace unexpectedly. Figuring that he was just having some fun, Sabrina relaxed for a moment.

"After all this time, you still can't call me by my real name." Quizmaster floated down to her and Salem, without having to hitch a ride on any of the now identified flying objects.

"I'm sorry," Sabrina said. "But you just don't look like an Albert."

"I'll be sure to tell my parents you said that."

"You have parents?" Sabrina asked.

"Well, I certainly wasn't hatched." He had finally reached them. "So, you don't call, you don't write—"

"I know, I know ... I don't send flowers," Sabrina completed his sentence.

"Well, I was going to say you don't pop by to see me, but now that you mention it—"

"I'm sorry," she said. "But I've been busy. I did finally get my Witch's License. By the way, thanks for forgetting to tell me about the whole family secret thing."

"Hey, I don't make up the rules, I just follow them," Quizmaster said.

"I hate to break up this warm reunion," Salem interrupted. "But what are we doing here?"

"Oh, you." Quizmaster acted as if he was

noticing Salem for the first time. "I forgot how annoying you could be."

"You try wearing the same fur outfit all year long and see how much fun you are at parties," Salem replied.

"Good point," Quizmaster said. "How do you like my new threads?" He modeled his outfit for them.

Quizmaster always had the most colorful wardrobe Sabrina had ever seen. This outfit was no different. Neon-blue top with purple polka dots and yellow pants with red Christmas lights wrapped around the legs. Subtle was apparently not part of his vocabulary.

"It's certainly festive," Sabrina said hopefully. "Are we going to a party?"

"I am," he replied, his Christmas lights blinking as he moved. "I figured I'll make an appearance at your sorority shindig since you'll be otherwise engaged."

"Doing what?" Sabrina asked warily.

"Finding your way through the Amazing Maze."

"Oh, great," Salem said. "I should have known by the rainbow doors."

Sabrina looked at the cat, then back to Quizmaster, apparently the only one in the galaxy who had never heard of the Amazing Maze. "And that would be?"

"Where you are now," Quizmaster replied.

Sabrina looked around but still only saw the vastness of space. She looked down the path, but it only went along a straight route with no twists or turns or even walls.

"I hate to point this out," Sabrina said. "But there's no maze in your maze."

"You always did take everything at face value," Quizmaster said. "You have to think beyond the space. Right now you're in the exact center of the maze. You have three hours to find your way out."

"But why?" Sabrina asked.

"You abused the power of the Magic Cue Ball."

"Wait. I'm stuck here just because I asked a few too many questions?"

Salem backed away, trying to go unnoticed.

He was unsuccessful.

"Hold it, cat." Sabrina picked him up by the scruff of his neck. "Since you apparently know so much about this place, why don't you explain to me why you're here, too."

Salem had a sheepish grin on his face. "Well, you know how there are only three questions allowed?"

"Yes."

"Well, since you went to class and weren't using it . . ."

"You asked the Cue Ball the third question." Sabrina filled in the blanks. "But you told me the Magic Cue Ball would stop glowing when the magic ran out. Why was it still glowing when I got back from my classes? I know you didn't wait all day before you decided to use it."

"True, I didn't wait all day to *use* it," Salem

said trying to pull himself away from Sabrina. "But I did wait all day to leave it."

"Just a second," Sabrina said, dropping Salem to the ground. "If he went over the five-minute time limit, then why am I here?"

"Need I remind you of the little run-on sentence you created?" Quizmaster asked.

"And it sent us here because of that?" Sabrina asked, miffed.

"The two of you overloaded a sensitive piece of magical equipment," Quizmaster said. "But, don't worry, it happens all the time. That's the problem with indecisive people. They never know when to stop asking questions and start listening to themselves."

"And now we're stuck in this maze just because you couldn't figure out what to do," Salem added.

"Hey, it's your fault we're here, too," Sabrina reminded him.

"Don't blame me," Salem said. "I knew what I wanted to do. And this so wasn't it."

"So, now what?" Sabrina asked. "And what are you doing here, by the way?"

"Quizmasters have to work the maze for one week out of every year," he said. "It's in our contracts. You just happened to luck out and get sent here during my week."

"And since you're my friend, you're going to help us, right?" Sabrina asked, although she already knew the answer.

"Sorry, no can do," Quizmaster replied. "I'm only here to start you off."

Again, Sabrina looked around the room. "Start me off, where?"

"On the Amazing Maze."

"We've covered that," Sabrina said. "I meant, how do we start? Do we just go down this path until we find a maze?"

"First the rules," Quizmaster said.

"How did I know there were going to be rules?" Sabrina asked sarcastically.

Knowing her well enough, Quizmaster didn't bother to answer her. Instead, he took on a formal tone, as if he were making a proclamation, which, technically, he was. "One. You must complete the maze in three hours' time."

"Or what?" Sabrina immediately asked.

"Patience never was one of your strong points," Quizmaster commented, and then slipped back into his official voice. "Two. If you do not complete the maze in three hours, you will be trapped in the maze forever."

"Great," Sabrina said, looking at Salem. "And me without a wristwatch."

"Hey, don't look at me. I don't even have wrists," the cat reminded her.

Quizmaster pointed into the air, and a grandfather clock appeared. The hour, minute, and second hands were all pointing directly at twelve.

"We managed to get this clock cheap at your aunts' going-out-of-business sale," Quizmaster said, referring to the clock shop Hilda and Zelda had owned before it went bankrupt.

"I thought it looked familiar," Sabrina said.

"And Three," Quizmaster continued in the official voice, "along the way, you will be quizzed. Solve the puzzles correctly, and you will find your way out."

"You need a new theme," Sabrina said. "This quiz thing is getting a little old."

"Occupational hazard, when your job title is Quizmaster," he responded. "Are you ready to begin?"

Sabrina held up her pointing finger to him. "What about my magic?"

"No magic in the maze," he said. "Can't have you popping home as soon as you start."

"That's a shocker," Sabrina said, returning her pointing finger to its holster in her pocket. "When does the clock start?"

"As soon as you choose the route into the maze," Quizmaster said.

"And how do we do that?" Sabrina asked.

"Well, little lady, let me tell you." Now Quizmaster's voice took on the tone of a game-show host. "To begin the Amazing Maze, will you choose Door Number One, Door Number Two, or Door Number Three?"

Sabrina watched as the three rainbow doors each flew together about fifty yards away from her. Stopping, they hovered next to each other. "Which is which? They all look the same."

"That's for you to decide," Quizmaster said.

"Well, since they all look the same," Sabrina said, watching as the portraits continued to fly past the doors, "maybe we should just take the one in the middle."

Quizmaster stood tall, motioning toward the center door. "The little lady has—"

"Or we could take the one on the left." Sabrina changed her mind. "I guess that would be Door Number One. Or would that be too obvious? Maybe we should go for Door Number Three. That's the last one, right? Or maybe that's too obvious."

Since Sabrina was not even giving him a chance to respond, Quizmaster looked darkly at Salem. "This is not a good start."

Chapter 5

☆

"**O**kay, fine. We'll take the one in the middle," Sabrina said firmly, hoping that she wouldn't change her mind again.

Salem perked up. "Finally."

Then Sabrina changed her mind. "Or maybe we should—"

"No!" Salem said firmly. "You made your choice. We're sticking to it. I don't plan to be here all day."

"You weren't exactly helping." Sabrina looked back at the doors, aware that both the Quizmaster and Salem were still waiting for her. "Fine. The middle door it is."

"Let the clock begin NOW," Quizmaster said in his official voice. The words echoed through space, and all the portraits froze in place while the second hand on the grandfather clock began to move.

"Admit it. You get a kick out of doing that," Sabrina said.

"Yeah, I do get a little thrill," Quizmaster confirmed. "Now it's time for you two to start this thing."

"How do we get to the door?" Sabrina asked.

The door she had chosen, along with its counterparts, continued to hover about one hundred fifty feet away from the path and Sabrina. Since the portraits had stopped moving when Quizmaster started the clock, there was nothing for Sabrina to hitch a ride on, either.

"Jump." Quizmaster said matter-of-factly.

Sabrina didn't need to measure the exact distance to know he was suggesting an impossible task. "I can't jump that far."

"Just push your feet off the floor in the direction of the door you chose. The antigravity of space will take care of the rest." The Quizmaster took a mirror out of his back pocket to check his reflection. "Now, if you'll excuse me, I have a party to get to."

With a flourish and a flash, he disappeared.

Sabrina looked back at the door in the distance. For the first time she noticed that the Amelia Earhart portrait was floating directly above it. Taking its positioning as a good sign, Sabrina readied herself for the jump.

"Come on," Sabrina said to Salem. She put out her arms and he jumped up into them. "Here goes nothing."

Sabrina bent down to give herself some extra propulsion, then sprang forward to the door. She flew through space toward the middle door while all the hovering portraits moved out of her way. Halfway to the door, Sabrina realized her mistake. Holding Salem in both arms, she wouldn't be able to reach for the doorknob. The two of them would probably slam right into it while it remained closed.

"What are you doing?" Salem asked as she shifted him around in her arms, trying for a better grasp.

"Trying to get a hand free," she replied as she shoved him under her left arm. It wasn't pretty, and certainly not comfortable for Salem, but she was able to reach for the doorknob with her right hand just in time. Giving the knob a little turn, Sabrina used the force of her jump to push herself and Salem through the door.

A flood of rainbow lights greeted them on the other side of the door as they were pulled forward with increasing speed. Sabrina couldn't see anything around her but the blur of lights. Not knowing where the tunnel of light would end, Sabrina was afraid that she and Salem would slam into a wall or something.

It took a few minutes before they began to slow, which Sabrina took to mean they were nearing their destination. A good thing, too, because she was starting to get a little airsick. A flash of color blinded her momentarily and when

Sabrina opened her eyes, she saw a long white hallway that looked like it stretched on for miles in front of her and Salem. Sabrina turned to find a white wall behind her. There were no rainbow doors or rainbow lights to be seen.

With the wall to her back, white walls to the side, and a white floor beneath her, it was a rather stark-looking maze she and Salem found themselves in. They could only go forward, and that direction didn't look like it had any twists or turns or any alternate routes at all. It was nothing more than one long hallway.

"Some maze this turned out to be," Sabrina said, gently dropping Salem to the ground. "I wouldn't exactly call it Amazing."

"It'll take us three hours just to get to the first turn," Salem said. "There has to be some kind of trick."

"Why do you say that?" Sabrina asked. "It could be some weird kind of endurance test. To see how long it takes to get to the real maze part of the maze."

"This is the Other Realm, Sabrina, not the army." Salem reminded her as he looked for anything odd nearby. "There's always a trick."

"Good point." Sabrina felt along the wall. "Try looking for a secret door or wall or something."

Salem brushed his body along the wall to no avail. "At my height, this will take forever. How I long for the days when I stood on only two legs."

"How I long for the days when you didn't

hack up hairballs all over my clothes." Sabrina gave up patting the wall. "It could take us forever to find a secret passage and we only have three hours. I say we start walking."

"Fine with me," Salem said.

"Just keep looking for anything out of the ordinary on the walls or in the floor. Anything that could be another route."

Together, they began the long trek down the seemingly endless hallway. Two sets of eyes scanned the walls and floor. Naturally, Salem took the lower half of the hall to examine while Sabrina took the higher half. As they continued down the hall, they found no hidden doors, no trap floors, or anything else that would qualify as another path. Lacking all other options, they continued along the path.

After what Sabrina assumed was several minutes of walking, still nothing out of the ordinary stood out and they appeared to be no closer to the end of the hall. She was glad that, of all the things that had happened to her so far, she had the good fortune of wearing her most comfortable shoes. All things considered, dressing in jeans and a light sweater, Sabrina had picked out a great outfit to wear while navigating a long maze. This was a good thing because she knew that once they did find a turn, she and Salem would most likely get a lot of exercise in the two hours and however many minutes of maze yet to come.

"This is ridiculous," Sabrina said as they continued to walk. "A maze with no turns makes absolutely no sense at all."

"No, this is the Other Realm," Salem reminded her and stopped. "This makes perfect sense."

"Why are you stopping?" Sabrina asked.

"We're going about this all wrong," he replied. "We have to treat this like any other Other Realm problem."

"How?"

"By using magic," he said, as if the answer had been obvious all along.

Sabrina couldn't believe her ears. "Weren't you paying attention? Quizmaster said I couldn't use my magic. If I could just navigate a magical maze with magic, what would be the point . . . however . . ."

The look in Sabrina's eyes caught Salem's attention immediately.

"However?" he prodded hopefully.

"However," she continued, forming an idea to help them out, "we should treat this maze like it's magic."

"That's what I meant," Salem said with a cocky tone in his voice. "But how?"

"Salem, what's the one thing that has been true about almost every spell that I've ever cast?"

"They usually go wrong, ending in some kind of disaster."

Sabrina gave him a look that said that was not the answer she was looking for. "No. Most of the spells I've cast were based on some pun or something with two different meanings. Like the time I had to actually open a can of worms to make my life a little more exciting."

"Your point?" Salem asked.

"This maze must represent something," Sabrina said. "Like my not being able to make decisions."

"I thought that was obvious," Salem said.

"No, I mean, it literally represents that," Sabrina said. "There are no turns because I'm not ready for them."

"So then, how do you *get* ready for them?" Salem asked.

Sabrina heard soft music playing behind them. It was so far away that she couldn't quite make out the tune, but it was definitely some kind of brass band playing. She couldn't imagine where the music was coming from since she already knew there was nothing in that direction.

Salem looked up at her as he pointed himself in the direction of the music. "Well, what are we waiting for?"

"There's nothing back there," Sabrina said, looking down the hall but still seeing only the hall.

The music stopped.

Sabrina wisely continued her thought. "Or there *was* nothing back there until I was ready to see it."

The music began again.

"That's it!" she said, moving toward the music. "The maze didn't show itself to me until I was ready for it."

"But I was ready for it," Salem said.

"Yeah, but you didn't cast the Magic Cue Ball spell," Sabrina reminded him. She was beginning to make some sense out of the Amazing Maze.

The music grew louder as Sabrina and Salem ran toward it. Sabrina could now tell that it was some kind of carnival music. It sounded exactly like the music she heard on the merry-go-round the last time the carnival had come to Westbridge.

The music was at its loudest when they came to an intersection.

"This wasn't here before," Sabrina said, referring to the two new paths.

"I say we don't question it," Salem said as he pointed a paw to the hall on their right. "The music is coming from this direction."

Sabrina scooped him up and made the turn. "Let's go."

As soon as she rounded the corner, Sabrina stopped in her tracks.

"Ladies and gentlemen, step right up!" a man in a carnival barker's outfit said to them.

Sabrina couldn't believe her eyes. "Mr. Kraft!"

"That's right, that's right! Ladies and gentlemen and children of all ages . . . and cats, too! Step right up!"

Standing ten feet in front of them, in a hallway that wasn't there a few minutes ago, stood Sabrina's high school principal. Dressed in a red-and-white-striped shirt, white pants, and a straw hat, he looked the part of the carnival barker standing behind a makeshift podium. He was holding a long stick and using it to point out a red curtain that covered the rest of the path.

Even more surprising was the carnival showgirl who stood beside Mr. Kraft twirling a baton. It was Libby Chessler, Sabrina's old rival, dressed in her Westbridge cheerleading outfit complete with a tiara with a big green feather sticking out of it.

Sabrina stared at her former arch nemesis. It had been almost two years since they had last seen each other. Libby's parents had transferred her to boarding school for their senior year of high school. At the time Sabrina thought that the wicked cheerleader was out of her life forever. She was even beginning to forget all the torment that Libby and her unfriendly clique had put her through.

"What are you doing here?" Sabrina asked before her natural instincts took over. "In my *dream.* What are you doing in my *dream?* Are you *dreaming,* too?" Convincing people that they were dreaming was an old standby for explaining magic. Sabrina had used it on many occasions in the past.

"See the Seven Wonders of the Other Realm, right behind this curtain," Mr. Kraft continued in carnival barker-speak. "See the cat who was once a man. See the girl who can't make up her mind. See the . . ."

"Okay, okay, we get the point," Sabrina said, walking up to the podium. "What is going on here? And why are you two involved?"

Salem walked around the podium and batted his paw at Mr. Kraft's leg, passing right through it. "It's okay, Sabrina. They're not real. They're holograms."

"Really?" Sabrina waved her hand in front of the Mr. Kraft but got no response. Immediately she stepped over to Libby, crossing way into her personal space. Expecting to hear Libby call her a freak or something, Sabrina was delighted when the cheerleader did nothing but continue to twirl her baton.

Sabrina had a mischievous grin. "This could be fun. I've always wanted to tell Libby a few things."

"We don't have time for that." Salem started for the curtain, but after a twirl and a swing, he found his path blocked—and his head nearly clobbered—by Libby's baton. "Or we could stick around for a few minutes."

The Mr. Kraft hologram came back to life. "Come see what's behind the curtain. Admission for the low, low price of one answer."

"One answer?" Sabrina asked. "To what question?"

Salem backed away from the baton and joined Sabrina at the podium. Holo-Libby resumed her twirling routine as if nothing had happened.

Mr. Kraft continued with the first puzzle of the maze. "Okay, little lady . . . what creature walks on four legs in the morning, two legs in the after-noon, and three legs at twilight?"

"I've heard that before," Sabrina said, scanning her memory for where she knew that question. "It's the riddle of the Sphinx! The answer is—"

"Wait!" Salem yelled as he sprang up to the podium, placing himself between Sabrina and Mr. Kraft. "Don't say it," he whispered to her urgently.

"But, Salem, I know it," she whispered back. "The answer is humans. As babies, we crawl on all fours, as children and adults, we walk on two legs, and as senior citizens we walk with a cane . . . which isn't exactly politically correct to assume, but it probably was back in the time of the Sphinx. Salem, it's an old puzzle, and if the rest of the maze is like this, then we're going to be fine."

"Once again, you're thinking like you're in the Mortal Realm," Salem said, no longer whispering.

"Time is running out, little lady," Mr. Kraft bellowed.

"Please stop calling me little lady," Sabrina said. "It's just too weird hearing it coming from you."

Salem turned to the hologram. "The answer is the Purple Spotted Nivik."

"Salem, are you crazy?" Sabrina yelled.

"Correct!" Mr. Kraft said. "Libby, show the folks what they've won."

Libby threw her baton high into the air to where it almost hit the ceiling. She twirled with a flourish and caught the baton as it returned. She then held out the baton and used it to pull back the curtain.

The darkness behind the curtain made it impossible to see what was beyond.

"The Purple Spotted Nivik?" Sabrina asked Salem as she picked him up into her arms.

"A member of the magicium class of animals,"

Salem explained. "I used to be an Other Realm zookeeper in one of my many areas of employment before I realized that ruling the world was the only job that would truly make me happy."

Sabrina walked toward the curtain, passing the wordless Libby. "You know, I think I prefer you quiet like this."

Using her baton as a weapon, Libby pushed Sabrina, roughly, through the curtain.

"Then again, maybe not," Sabrina said as she stumbled to the other side.

Sabrina put Salem down as the curtain closed behind them. Suddenly the ceiling lit up, and she saw a dozen different hallways going off in all directions.

When Sabrina looked over her shoulder, she found that the curtain was gone. In its place were a dozen *more* hallways leading to all sorts of destinations. Sabrina thought she had trouble picking three doors; now she had twenty-four routes open to her!

"Well, you said you wanted twists and turns," Salem said.

"Great."

Chapter 6

Sabrina stared at the many doors and thought about the possible combinations. "I could pick a number and then choose the matching door. Or I could count from the right and stop . . . when? The fourth door? The fifth? Or the middle door?" Sabrina was paralyzed.

"Pick one in the next century," Salem said with a yawn. "Here's an idea—let's just pick the closest one."

Sabrina started walking down the path closest to where she was standing, heading to the nearest door. Though she didn't know if she was getting any closer to the end of the maze, the mere fact that she was finally able to turn right and left in the giant puzzle made her feel as if she was getting somewhere. Of course, all the turns looked the same to Sabrina, that is, until the floor began to change.

73

"What's this?" Sabrina asked. The floor was sectioned into colorful blocks. As she walked, Sabrina noticed that each block had either a red, orange, yellow, green, blue, or purple square in its center. The blocks continued one after the other, down the hall.

"I hope this is a sign that we're going in the right direction," Salem said, sniffing the air. "A definite sign we're going the right way."

Salem took off, his nose leading the way. Though dogs were generally better known for their heightened sense of smell, Sabrina had learned to trust Salem's since it usually meant there was food near. And Sabrina hoped that if there was food, there was somebody making the food who could point them in the right direction to get out of the less-than-Amazing Maze.

Sabrina had to run full out to keep up with Salem. The cat was moving so quickly that he was actually leaping over some of the colored blocks. Sabrina was so intent on making sure that Salem did not run out of her sight that she did not notice that the walls were changing. The hallway was getting wider and splotches of bright colors appeared on the walls. The whole maze seemed to be taking on a different look. Although Sabrina didn't notice the visual changes, she certainly couldn't miss the smells that Salem had picked up on earlier.

Scents of sugar and spice and everything nice permeated the maze. Salem continued to run toward the source when Sabrina suddenly stopped short, nearly toppling over. She pulled at her feet, but they wouldn't budge. Something was holding on to her and keeping her stuck to the ground.

"Salem, help!" she yelled.

Up ahead, Salem skidded to a halt. "But we're so close!"

"I'm stuck on something." But Sabrina couldn't tell what she was stuck on. Under her feet, she just saw a red block like the other blocks she had been running past. However, looking closer, Sabrina noticed a black blob sticking out from under her left shoe.

Salem trotted back to her. "What's wrong?"

"I can't move." Sabrina tried lifting her feet to show him what she meant and, obviously, couldn't budge them. "See."

"Is that all?" Salem asked as he circled her feet, careful not to step on the red part of the square.

"How do I get out of this?" Sabrina asked.

"Just wait," Salem said.

"For what?"

"Nothing. Just wait."

"Salem, this is ridiculous." Sabrina tried pulling at her feet. "Try to get something to pry my feet looosee. . . ." She toppled over as the red block released her.

"I told you to wait." Salem began licking her left shoe.

Sabrina pulled her feet away from him. "What were you doing? That was disgusting."

"No, that's a sugary treat," Salem said. "Come on, there's more where that came from."

And again the cat was off.

Salem was running ahead. Sabrina was careful to walk more slowly, now that she knew to look out for the squares with the black dots. *Let him get stuck next time,* she thought.

Now that she had time to look around and get her bearings, Sabrina noticed that this part of the maze looked different. As Sabrina followed Salem, she noted there were pictures of candy, lollipops, and other sweet treats decorating the walls.

Then the signs began.

> THIS WAY TO TAFFY WOODS
> WATCH OUT FOR GOOEY GUMBALLS
> TOUR THE CHOCOLATE MOUNTAIN

Sabrina's curiosity grew as the corridor finally opened up into an indoor world of candies and sweets. She was in a giant cavern in the maze, bigger than a football stadium. It was filled with a child's dream of chocolate and taffy and anything else that could be imagined.

There was one final sign that Sabrina read aloud. "Welcome to Candy . . . world?"

Up ahead, she saw Salem nibbling on what appeared to be flowers made out of cotton candy surrounded by a rock candy garden. This all seemed vaguely familiar to Sabrina. "Salem, I'm assuming the Magic Eight Ball wasn't the only Other Realm idea you sold to a toy company?"

"I don't know . . . what you're . . . talking about," Salem said between munches, acting innocently, but not convincingly.

Up ahead, Sabrina saw that the path wound its way through Candyworld.

A white chocolate river wound past Sabrina. She traced it back to a small chocolate mountain far off in the distance of the Candyworld cavern. To her left stood a forest made of licorice trees. She figured that the Taffy Woods mentioned on one of the signs was probably near. To her right was a chocolate-chip cookie sculpture that Salem was eyeing as he munched on the pink flowers.

Sabrina realized her day had been so crazy that she hadn't eaten since the hurried lunch she had in one of her alternate futures. She eyed the candy and treats with her mouth drooling. Salem seemed to be enjoying himself snacking away, but she knew better than to take candy from strangers or strange lands. Passing up the sweet treats, Sabrina continued down the path.

"Salem, come on," she called.

"But, Sabrina!" Salem pleaded from the garden.

"We've got to move." Even though she didn't have a watch, Sabrina was sure they were coming up on the first hour and that time was running out.

Knowing she was right, Salem reluctantly pulled himself away, but only after biting off another mouthful of cotton candy and munching on it as he walked.

Sabrina continued along the maze, watching the ground for any more of those squares with the black dots. "Why aren't there any turns in this part of the maze?"

"Beats me," Salem said. "I didn't design this place."

"Watch out." Sabrina jumped over the square.

Sabrina stopped short on the path. She wasn't stuck this time, just struck with an idea. She put out a hand to stop Salem, who had kept walking ahead. "Wait a minute. Were you in this maze before?"

"Um . . . well . . ." Salem wouldn't look her in the eyes. "Yes."

"Why didn't you say something!" she yelled. "You can lead us out of here."

"No, I can't," he explained. "Aside from the fact that it's been more than fifty years since I was stuck here, this place changes every three hours. That's why we have the time limit. The halls are nowhere near where they used to be. I don't know how to get out."

"Still, you could have said something," Sabrina said.

Salem just looked at the ground, shaking his head and mumbling something Sabrina couldn't understand.

"What?" She asked, picking him up.

Salem turned his head, too ashamed to look

right at her. "It was too embarrassing," he muttered.

Sabrina had trouble imagining him embarrassed about anything. "After all the embarrassing things you've seen me do since I moved in with you and my aunts, you're too afraid to tell me about something that happened more than fifty years ago?"

Salem's entire face lit up. "Hey, you're right. You have done some pretty stupid things. Like the time—"

"Salem!" Sabrina quickly interrupted, putting him back down on the ground. "We're talking about you here. Not me."

"Oh, all right," he said. "It was back in the early days of my movement to take over the world. I had so many plans and so few followers. So I used magic to pass along my orders to the operatives in the field."

Sabrina sat down on a purple square, giving her feet a rest while Salem told his tale.

"There were magic messages flying all around the Other Realm. One minute troops would get orders to do one thing, and before they could move, a completely contradictory order would arrive. I had witches crossing between realms, darting off into space, and going anywhere and everywhere. Before I knew it, my meager minions were hopelessly lost."

"Where does the Magic Cue Ball come in?" Sabrina asked.

"It was still the Magic Eight Ball back then,"

Salem reminded her. "With dozens of witches lost doing countless tasks I had forgotten I had given them, and only allowed three questions to ask. . . . You do the math."

Sabrina thought back to the six classes the Magic Cue Ball helped her pick earlier. "Be creative?"

"Too creative," Salem said. "Kind of like asking it one huge run-on sentence."

Sabrina remembered her own failed creativity that got her stuck in the maze.

BONG!

A bell roused them out of storytime.

Sabrina spun to see her aunts' old grandfather clock in the middle of the path. The hour hand was on the one. They only had two hours left to get through the maze before it changed on them and they would be stuck inside forever.

"We'd better get going," she said, getting up from the ground.

"My thoughts exactly," Salem agreed.

As soon as they passed the clock, Sabrina noticed a rainbow bridge on the right side of the path. The bridge stretched over a caramel lake so large that she had trouble seeing to the other side. "Where does this go?"

"I don't know," Salem said. "The last time I was here it was a shortcut. The path will wind around the lake, but it gets us near to the end much faster."

"Are you sure?" Sabrina asked.

"No," Salem admitted.

"What if they changed this part of the maze? Where will we end up?" worried Sabrina.

For once the cat had no answer.

"I guess we'll just have to try it and see," Sabrina said reluctantly as she stepped up onto the rainbow bridge.

The pair started their way across the caramel lake. To Sabrina's surprise, the bridge did not collapse in the middle, end abruptly, or dump them in the lake at all. Instead, after a few minutes of walking, it led them safely to a new part of the multicolored path that Sabrina hoped was near the end.

"Looks like you made a good decision," Salem said. Sabrina sighed with relief as they were about ten feet from the end of the bridge. "I was half expecting to hear some troll who lived under the bridge yell out—"

"Who's up there on my bridge?!" a deep scratchy voice bellowed from beneath their feet.

"I was expecting something with more of a rhyme, but—" Sabrina looked to Salem for an explanation.

Salem stopped and looked up at Sabrina. "That's new."

Sabrina stayed where she was, ten feet from the end, afraid to move forward for fear of the troll. She knew from first-hand experience that trolls tended to be more of an annoyance than a threat, but they were a persistent annoyance. Standing frozen on the bridge, Sabrina naturally thought of

Roland, the first troll she had ever met. Roland had a habit of popping up in her life and causing all sorts of havoc trying to get Sabrina to fall in love with him. It all started when he did a job for her and demanded her hand in marriage as payment. Now, Sabrina worried what the troll underneath them would want as a fee for crossing his bridge.

The voice bellowed again. "Who's up there on my bridge!"

Timidly Sabrina stepped to the edge, peering over. She saw nothing but the caramel lake. "Sorry. We were just passing by. Didn't know anyone lived here. If you don't mind, we'll just continue on our way."

Sabrina looked at Salem and they started to move. Before they got one step, the voice again chimed in, "Who's up there on my bridge?"

Sabrina turned back to the edge of the bridge, still seeing nothing under her. "I guess he wants to know who's on his bridge."

"I'd say that's a safe assumption," Salem said.

"I'm Sabrina Spellman," she yelled down to the lake, "and I'm with Salem—"

Salem distracted her by rapidly shaking his head back and forth. "It's best not to use my last name around here. Never know who we might run into."

"Someday you're going to have to tell me every single thing you did before you were turned into a cat," Sabrina said. "I'm getting tired of these surprises."

Once again the voice bellowed. "Who's up there on my—"

"Oh, knock it off," another voice said from behind Sabrina.

When she turned, Sabrina saw a head popping up through the rainbow bridge. The troll was coming up through a trapdoor that swung back, crashing onto the bridge with a bang. As Sabrina watched more and more of the troll coming up from under the bridge, she had to admit she liked what she saw. He looked to be about her age, almost six feet tall, with blond hair and blue eyes. This was like no troll she had ever seen before.

"Sorry about that," the troll-boy said in a voice that was deep but certainly not scratchy. "The voice is an automatic alarm that came with the place. I've been meaning to get it removed."

Not expecting to find such a cute guy in the maze, Sabrina was momentarily speechless.

"So, Sabrina Spellman and Salem with-no-last-name." The troll-boy flashed a smile at the cat. "I'm Toby. Toby, the troll."

"You're a troll?" She finally managed to regain her speech.

Another cute smile flashed across his face. "Let me guess, you've been reading those fairy stories where we're all short little guys with horrible personalities."

"No!" Sabrina didn't want this guy to think she was ignorant. "It's just . . . I know a troll and he's nothing like you."

"Well, are all witches as cute as you?" he asked in a flirtatious tone.

Sabrina smiled, flattered by the compliment.

Salem broke the moment by pretending to cough up a hairball.

"So, who's this troll you know?" Toby asked.

"His name is Roland," Sabrina said with a roll of her eyes, indicating that Roland was not exactly a friend.

"I think I know him," Toby said. "Short guy? Can't hold down a job?"

Sabrina laughed at the description. "That would be him."

"Yeah, he tends to give us trolls a bad name," Toby said as he motioned back to his trapdoor leading under the bridge. "Why don't you two stop in and join me downstairs?"

Sabrina was very tempted by the offer, but knew she had to refuse. "We have this time limit."

"But no one ever wants to stop in," he persisted. "And I'm all alone in my big empty place."

Sabrina looked down at the bridge. She couldn't image his place being all that big since the bridge wasn't all that wide. Then again, Sabrina stopped questioning Other Realm logic long ago.

"I was just making lunch," he added. "It's real food, not just the candy snacks all around here."

Sabrina's stomach was certainly tempted, and she didn't have to look at Salem to know he was interested, too. "Well, maybe for a few minutes."

"Great," Toby said, his face beaming. "Come right down."

Sabrina looked into the trapdoor and saw a flight of stairs that led down to an enormous room. "Wow, great place. When I get out of here, you'll have to come visit me."

Toby's cute smile suddenly left his face. "I'm kind of stuck here. I can't leave."

Sabrina suddenly lost her appetite when she was reminded of the reason for the time limit. "Ever?"

"Oh, but I love it here," he said with his smile back on his face. "No responsibilities. Dozens of people pass by every week. Of course, none of them stop in. But some do come back every now and then. You know, when they get trapped in the maze."

Sabrina and Salem started backing away.

"Now that you mention it, we do have to get moving." Sabrina didn't want to be rude, but she didn't want to be stuck there forever, either. "I'm sorry."

"That's okay," Toby said, still smiling. "But feel free to come back if you don't get out."

"Thanks," Sabrina said, though she wasn't exactly hoping to get trapped in the maze. She gave him a little wave goodbye and then turned to walk to the end of the bridge. By the time they were back on the path, Sabrina had heard the trapdoor close. "That was—"

"The mother lode!" Salem broke in, awestruck. He took off at a run.

Sabrina immediately saw what he was racing toward. There was no way she could miss the giant gingerbread house with icing and candy decorating the walls and rooftop. This time Sabrina ran right after Salem.

"Stop," she urgently whispered as she reached Salem munching on the front stairs to the house.

"Wmfy?" Salem said, his mouth full of step.

After Sabrina figured out that he was asking her "why" he should stop, she pulled him away from the house.

"Remember the last time we came across a gingerbread house?" Sabrina asked. "A wicked witch kidnapped Harvey and tried to fatten him up to eat him." The memory wasn't pleasant for her, and not just because of the witch. Sabrina always felt a twinge when she thought about Harvey.

Salem finally swallowed the piece of house. "Sabrina, you can't just assume all gingerbread houses are owned by wicked witches. Didn't you learn anything from Toby the troll about stereotypes?"

Just then they heard voices from inside the house.

"Double, Double, soil and rubble."

"Cauldron burn and chocolate bubble."

"Hurry in or you'll be in a whole lot of distress."

Sabrina threw open the front door of the house. Normally, Sabrina would have been more cautious, but she knew those voices. Standing in front of her were three old friends: Jenny, Valerie, and Dreama.

"Dreama, you can still say the word *trouble*. It *is* part of the language. We just can't use it in reference to the game since that loser sold off the rights." Jenny hadn't noticed that Sabrina had come into the room yet.

"Oh, sorry. These magic rules always confuse me," Dreama said.

They were dressed in long black robes and pointy hats like witches wore in cartoons. Odd, since only one of the three was a witch. Odder still was that they did not stand around a cauldron. Instead, they were circling a big plastic dome that had a pair of dice inside it.

The Amazing Maze kept getting stranger and stranger.

Chapter 7

☆

"**H**i, Sabrina!" Valerie smiled in her typically excited manner.

This got Jenny and Dreama's attention. They both turned to Sabrina and waved hello.

Sabrina came into the house, which had as much candy inside as it had outside. Salem followed, munching every step of the way.

"What are you guys doing here?" Sabrina asked the trio.

"We're not really here," Valerie said, before adding, "I think."

"We're holograms," Dreama said.

"You mean like Mr. Kraft and Libby?" Sabrina asked.

Jenny nodded while Dreama asked, "Who's Libby?"

"You missed her," Sabrina said. "She went to boarding school before you got to Westbridge."

Valerie added more to the response. "She was so cool—"

"She was a total despot," Jenny interrupted. "She stood for all that was wrong with the social caste system of high school. Just because she let you on the second-string cheerleading squad doesn't make her cool, Valerie."

Sabrina's confusion suddenly grew. "Wait a minute. You three don't know each other. You all went to Westbridge at different times. How come you act like you're all friends?"

"We're holograms," Dreama said.

"Obviously this one needs some more programming," Salem said. "That seems to be her answer for everything."

Normally, Dreama would have been offended by the cat's little insult, but holo-Dreama just ignored him as if he weren't there. "And we have a test for you."

"It's not another silly question with a stupid answer, is it?" Sabrina asked.

"No. This is more of a challenge for your decision-making skills." Jenny seemed to be the official rule keeper for the group.

"Great. Just what we need," Salem said.

"Thanks for your vote of confidence," Sabrina said. "Come on, we can do this."

"The test is for you alone," Jenny added.

Sabrina shot Salem a look. "Don't say it."

Salem just smiled back at her, innocently.

"Okay, so what do I do?" Sabrina asked.

"Choose," the three witches responded. Then, together they chanted:

> *One for three,*
> *'Fore dice are done.*
> *Best friend will it be.*
> *Which is the one?*

Sabrina stood, speechless as her three holo-friends stared at her, waiting for some kind of response.

Finally Sabrina spoke. "What in the world did *that* mean?"

"Beats me," Dreama said.

"I knew she wouldn't get it," Valerie said to Jenny. "I didn't get it and I was saying it."

Okay, fine," Jenny said. "Basically, you need to make a simple choice. Of the three of us, whom did you consider to be your *best* friend?"

"And you have to choose before the dice roll to snake eyes," Valerie said, pointing to the dice under the plastic dome.

"Wait, I have to choose my one best friend out of the three of you?" Sabrina asked.

At her feet Salem whined, "We're never getting out of this maze."

"But how am I supposed to pick one?"

"That's for you to figure out before the dice hit snake eyes," Jenny explained.

Sabrina paused for a moment, looking at the dice and the plastic dome. "And how are you supposed to roll the dice under that?"

Together, the three girls leaned on the dome, pushing it down. When it popped back up, the dice inside jumped. Luckily, they landed on double sixes.

"I should have seen that coming," Sabrina said, mostly to herself.

"Tick, tick, tick," Salem prodded, reminding her that they didn't have much time.

Pop. Three and four. The dice reminded her of the same thing.

Feeling it would be better to move, Sabrina paced around the candy-strewn room. "Okay, I can figure this out. Jenny, you were the first person to be my friend when I moved to Westbridge, and that meant a lot to me. But, then Valerie, you were the first mortal I was allowed to tell that I was a witch, and that was great, too. Of course, Dreama, since you're a witch, I didn't have to keep any secrets from you, so that added to our friendship."

Pop. Two and six.

Sabrina kept going, both pacing and speaking faster. "But, Jenny, you just seemed to disappear, and Valerie, you moved away when you were supposed to stay, and Dreama you just left, too."

Pop. Three and five.

Sabrina tried a new tack. "Jenny, what's my favorite color?"

"Sorry, we can't take part in the decision-making process," Jenny replied.

Pop. One and two. Close.

"So, I guess asking you guys to pick a number between one and ten wouldn't work, either," Sabrina asked in desperation.

Pop. Five and five. No other response.

"Okay, then. I have no clue."

Pop. Two and four.

"I can't choose among you," wailed Sabrina. "What should I do?"

Pop.

Snake eyes.

"I'm sorry," Sabrina said to Salem, then she turned to her holo-friends. "Will you at least tell me who I should have chosen?"

"It was a trick question," Jenny explained. "When none of the options jump out as the best, you should think about choosing all of the above."

"That's not fair," Sabrina said right before the floor dropped out from underneath her and Salem.

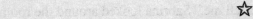

Chapter 8

Sabrina slid down a long dark chute, trying to grab on to anything to slow her descent. She couldn't see Salem, but every now and then she heard his claws scraping against the chute above her in his own attempt to slow his fall. Looking down between her feet, Sabrina saw nothing, but she did hear what sounded like a door opening beneath her. Bracing for impact, she prepared for the worst.

The chute deposited her about ten feet above the ground. The speed of her descent wound up knocking her on her rear. Shortly after, Salem landed with a thud. When Sabrina looked up, she saw that the chute that dropped them there had disappeared.

"Where are we?" Salem asked. He couldn't see for himself due to the fact that his face was scrunched into the ground.

"You tell me." Sabrina looked around the room and was amazed by what she saw. She and Salem had been dropped into a room that was about as big as her high school gym. The center of the room was empty, but along each of the walls were piles of the strangest collection of items she had ever seen. There were old car parts, rusted-out household appliances, a bathtub, a white picket fence, and even a kitchen sink. It was like they fell into the middle of an old junkyard.

"I've never been here before, but it smells slightly like cheese," Salem said after pulling his face off the floor and sniffing the air. "And I don't think we're alone."

Sabrina followed Salem's pointing paw with her eyes and saw another set of eyes staring back at her from the shadows in the junk along one of the walls. Then she noticed another pair off to the side staring at her just as intensely.

"Hello," she tentatively said, staying safely in the nicely lit center of the room.

"Hello," one of the voices answered back.

"Hello," the other one said.

"So glad we got that part covered," Salem mumbled at Sabrina's feet.

Sabrina ignored the cat and addressed her comments to the glowing eyes in the shadows. "I'm Sabrina, and this is Salem. Who are—"

"Cat!" boomed out from the darkness near one set of the glowing eyes.

"Cat!" echoed the other one.

"Looks like we've come across Tweedle Dumb and Tweedle Dumber," Salem said.

"Don't be rude," she whispered to him before returning her attention to the eyes. "Would you mind telling me what part of the maze we're in?"

"Rat," said one of the voices.

"Trap," said the other.

Sabrina was getting a little tired of the short responses. "Well, that explains the faint smell of cheese. And you two would be?"

"Rats!" Salem yelped as he ran to hide behind Sabrina's legs.

"Salem, knock it off," she said, trying to shoo him away. "Why are you hiding from a couple of rats?"

"Not just rats," he said, clinging tightly to her, "Other Realm rats."

On cue, the rats stepped from the shadows, and Sabrina instantly understood Salem's fear. Sabrina had forgotten about Other Realm rats. These two rats were as big as grown men, which made sense because they were grown men. Other Realm rats weren't really rats at all, but men and women dressed in rat costumes. Quizmaster's roommate was such a man-rat, although he wasn't as strange as the pair scurrying around in front of Sabrina right now.

One of the rats was gray while the other was white. Sabrina had never seen a white rat before, either regular or man-sized. Salem, however, looked as if he knew these types of rats very well and was very much afraid of them.

"Meow!" cried the white rat.

The gray rat echoed, "Meow."

They ran back and forth in front of Sabrina, pretending to swipe at Salem in a game of cat and mouse, or more specifically, rats and cat.

"I don't mean to interrupt your fun," Sabrina said to the two rats. "But do either of you know the way out of this room?"

"No way out," said gray.

"No way out," said white.

Somewhere, behind the walls of junk, Sabrina heard a door slide open. The two rats froze in their tracks at the sound.

Salem was scrabbling at Sabrina's legs, so she bent down to pick him up. When she straightened up, the rats were gone.

"Where'd they go?" she asked, but then realized they were hovering together in one of the corners of the room. "What's going on?"

"Rat Trap!" the rats yelled in unison, pointing high up on the wall.

Sabrina looked to where they were pointing and saw a hole in the wall that must have been the sliding door that just opened.

"Can we get out that way?" she asked the rats.

They didn't respond. They just stayed huddled in the corner.

"Salem, do you think you could climb—" Sabrina was cut off when she noticed a bowling ball roll out of the hole. "How strange."

She watched the bowling ball as it rolled along the junk as if it were on roller-coaster tracks. The bowling ball rolled up over the pipes and down into the bathtub before falling out through a hole in the center of the tub. It dropped to the ground, knocking over a floor lamp, which fell onto an old tire, pushing it away. Sabrina was mesmerized as the tire rolled past her and Salem and knocked into a table on the other side of the room. A car bumper on top of the table tipped over and knocked into the picket fence. The fence did a tumble and the pointy end landed on a rope, splitting it in half. Sabrina's eyes followed up the rope to the ceiling of the room.

That's when she noticed the cage dropping from above her.

"Hold on!" she yelled to Salem as she ducked. The cage came down around the pair. When she stood up, she found that they were stuck in the cage. "Trapped, like . . . oh, I get it now."

The gray and white rats had come out from their corner and were now circling around the cage.

"Ha ha! We're still free!" said the white rat.

Sabrina and Salem looked to the gray rat, waiting for him to echo his friend.

"What?" the gray rat asked the pair.

"Aren't you going to say—" Sabrina stopped herself. She didn't really care for an explanation. "Can you help get us out of here?"

The gray one laughed. "Get you out? If we get you out—"

"—then we could get caught," the white one completed the thought. "As long as you're trapped inside—"

"—we're safe outside," said gray.

"I think I liked them better when they were repeating each other," Sabrina said, looking at the bars. "Salem, why don't you crawl through the bars and see if you can get help."

"Yes, Salem—" started gray.

"—crawl through the bars," finished white with a gleam in his eyes.

"Uh-uh. No way," the cat said, clinging to Sabrina for dear life.

"This is ridiculous," Sabrina said. "How are we expected to get out of this maze if it keeps trapping us places?"

"Don't make mistakes—" said white.

"Don't get trapped," said gray.

"Are you guys going to help us or make fun of us?" Sabrina asked.

"C. All of the above," they replied in unison.

"All of the above?" That sounded slightly familiar to Sabrina. "Are we here because I couldn't choose between my three best friends?"

"Bing! Bing! Bing! Bing! Bing!" The two rats made sounds indicating that she was right.

"Great, now we've moved on to sound effects," Salem said.

The two rats lunged toward the cage, causing the cat to clutch on to Sabrina tightly.

"Wait a minute," Salem said as he let go and jumped down from her arms. "If I can't get out, they can't get in. This could be fun."

"Salem, don't torment the rats," Sabrina said. "We have more important things to figure out."

"I can think and torment at the same time." Salem paraded around the cage, daring the rats to try and grab him while staying just out of arm's reach.

"Okay, do what you want to do while I try to get us out of here," Sabrina said.

Minutes passed and Sabrina couldn't come up with a single idea on how to get out of the cage. She had tried lifting it up, but it was too heavy, and Salem and the rats were too busy playing around to help her. The junk along the walls was too far away from her to reach, so she couldn't use anything to pry the bars apart. Stomping on the floor was useless, too. She had hoped that there was a trapdoor or something hollow beneath her, but it was just solid floor.

Sabrina slid down to the floor and sat down to watch Salem prance around inches from the rats' reach.

"Are you having fun?" She asked.

"You can't begin to imagine," he replied, chuckling. "I could do this all day."

"You could wind up doing this for the rest of your life," she reminded him. That thought brought her back to the problem at hand. "There has to be a logical way out of here."

"Work it out," said gray.

"Work it out," said white as he almost got a hold of Salem's tail.

Sabrina already felt as if she had worked everything out, but obviously there was some answer if even the rats knew it. She stood up to pace around the cage, careful not to step on Salem as he danced back and forth. "Okay. Why did the maze send us here?"

Not surprisingly, there was no answer.

Sabrina continued pacing, "We're here because I couldn't choose between my friends."

"Bing!! Bing!! Bi—"

"We got that part already," she silenced the rats. "But why couldn't I think to say that they were all my best friends? Why couldn't I make a decision?"

Salem and the rats stopped to look at her, waiting for an answer.

"Because I didn't want to hurt their feelings," she said and looked at the rats.

"Bing! Bing! Bing!"

"But they were only holograms," Salem reminded her.

"Yeah, but in my mind, they're real people," Sabrina reasoned. "When you're talking about your friends, sometimes you have to make new rules. I should have followed my instincts, and chosen all three."

"Bing! Bing! Bing!" the rats said happily,

while a look of excitement came across their faces. "That means . . ."

All around the room, the junk that had fallen magically shifted back into its original position until the cage around Sabrina and Salem slowly lifted back up to the ceiling.

"We're free!" Sabrina cheered.

But Salem wasn't cheering; he was hiding behind Sabrina.

"Lift me up! Lift me up!" he screamed.

His cries went unanswered as Sabrina disappeared.

Chapter 9

Sabrina found herself back in the normal part of the maze with boring white walls and floor. There were no colorful treats, rainbow bridges, or crazy rat-men. There was also no Salem.

"All right, I'm somewhere lost in the maze, and Salem is nowhere to be found," Sabrina said to herself as she started walking through the maze. "Can this day get any worse?"

Upon that, Sabrina turned a corner and found herself face to face with Harvey.

"I should have seen that one coming," she said before yelling out to whomever may have been listening. "Okay, this one really isn't fair. What did I do to deserve this?"

"I've been asking myself the same thing," Harvey said.

Sabrina was thrown off by what she assumed was a hologram being so direct with her. She reached out her hand and instead of passing through him, it stopped upon hitting solid flesh. "You're really here?!"

"Where is *here?*" Harvey asked. "I was just about to suit up for football practice and all of a sudden I'm not in the locker room anymore. I'm in this hallway. Sabrina, what's going on?"

"Would you believe that you're having a dream?" she asked out of desperation.

"Let's not start that again," he said.

"I didn't have anything to do with this," Sabrina said.

"You're the only person I know who can make people appear and disappear," Harvey said.

"Technically, that's not true," Sabrina said, thinking of all the other witches he had met while they were dating. "I'm here against my will, just like you are."

"Yeah, but you were raised where things like this are normal," he said.

"Again, technically incorrect," she said, before changing her strategy. "I don't want to fight about this."

"Then send me back to my school," Harvey said. "If I'm late to this practice, I may be cut from the team. The coach has been looking for a reason to get rid of me." He sighed.

"So, what are we doing here?"

"I don't know," Sabrina honestly replied. "I've

been trapped in this maze, and I guess you're another challenge I have to get past before I can get out."

Harvey moved to the side so that she could pass. "Well, don't let me get in your way."

Sabrina stayed where she was. "Somehow I don't think it will be that easy."

"Why?" he asked.

"This whole day has been about making decisions." Sabrina tried to reason out the logic, knowing she was about to tread on thin ice. "Maybe I'm supposed to convince you to change a decision *you* made."

Harvey didn't respond.

It was then that Sabrina noticed that he couldn't respond. She also noticed that he looked a little odd standing entirely still. Tentatively she gave him a little push. He didn't move. He was frozen in place.

Once again, Sabrina was frustrated that the Other Realm seemed intent on proving that her life was, in fact, as abnormal as they came.

That was when the Quizmaster popped in right next to her. "Boy, you college kids sure know how to throw a party. I haven't been at such a fun shindig since—"

Sabrina approached her former Quizmaster. "Why did you have to bring Harvey into this? Why couldn't you just use a hologram like all the others?

"Sabrina, it's all part of the maze. It wasn't my

idea to bring him here; the maze works of its own free will."

Sabrina softened. "Could you at least unfreeze him?"

Quizmaster reached out to her with his back still to the wall. "Yes, I can unfreeze him, but then I'd have to explain everything to the both of you. Since he's not a witch, he probably won't understand any of it and I'll have to explain it all again. And Sabrina, let's be honest, you're not getting through this maze all that quickly. Do you know how long you were stuck in that cage? We really don't have the time for long drawn out discussions."

"So I'm just supposed to stand here and ignore the fact that Harvey is frozen a few feet away from me?" Sabrina asked with sarcasm in her voice.

"No, he's serving his purpose," Quizmaster said. "For the next quiz you need a visual aid."

"For future reference," Sabrina said. "A photo would have worked just fine."

"If it's any consolation," Quizmaster said, "when he's returned to the Mortal Realm, I'll make sure he doesn't remember any of this."

"But you can't," Sabrina told him. "Spells like that won't work on him anymore. He passed the limit last year."

Sabrina was right. After all the magic Sabrina had used on him while they were dating, he had actually built up a resistance to it.

"This is one of those times I think I can get

special permission from the Witches' Council to bend the rules," Quizmaster said. "But only because Harvey's here against your will."

"Thank you," she said, looking at poor frozen Harvey.

"I don't mean to be rude," Quizmaster said, "but the clock is ticking."

With a wave of his hand, the grandfather clock appeared beside Sabrina.

BONG!

BONG!

Two hours down, one to go.

"Okay, so what's the quiz, riddle, or whatever you have for me now?" Sabrina asked.

"As you've already figured out," Quizmaster explained, "the maze represents all the indecision in your life."

"Ha! I was right!" Sabrina was bouncing up and down on her feet.

"Calm down, girl," Quizmaster said. "That was the easy part."

Sabrina stopped bouncing, properly chastised.

"Now the question is, if you could go back and change a decision you made, would you do it?"

Sabrina was back to being confused. "Such as . . . ?"

"Such as telling Harvey you're a witch before he had to find out the hard way," the Quizmaster offered.

"You mean I can go back in time and tell him I'm a witch before he finds out on his own."

Quizmaster gave her a smile. "It's an option."

"But what about my aunts?" Sabrina asked.

"How did they come into this?" Quizmaster asked.

"They would kill me if I ever told anyone I'm a witch," Sabrina said. "And my dad, too. And I know the Witches' Council won't be too crazy about it, either."

"But he already did find out on his own," Quizmaster reminded her.

"True . . ."

"But what do *you* want, Sabrina?"

Sabrina looked at poor frozen Harvey yet again. What *did* she want? She sighed and turned back to Quizmaster.

"I want to be with Harvey again," Sabrina said slowly. "But I can't just change schools. Or all of my plans. Especially now that I finally decided on my schedule for next semester."

With that, Harvey immediately disappeared.

"Hey, where did he go now?" Sabrina asked.

"Back to where he came from," Quizmaster said. "With no memory of what happened."

"Does that mean this is over?" Sabrina asked. "I mean, the maze can't do anything worse than bringing Harvey here."

"This little exercise isn't about hurting you, Sabrina," Quizmaster explained. "It's about helping you."

"Fine, I'm helped," she said. "Lesson over."

"Not yet," Quizmaster said and disappeared.

"That's it!" Sabrina yelled into the air, hoping he was still listening. "You're off my Christmas card list!"

Sabrina continued down the hall in a huff. She was stomping so hard and barely paying attention that she nearly stepped on Salem.

"Hey!" he yelled, jumping out of the way. "Watch it!'

"Salem!" She bent to pick up her traveling companion and noticed that his eyes seemed to be slightly glazed over. "What happened to you?"

"Oh, the horror," he said, with a shudder. "I'd rather not discuss it. What happened to you?"

"I'd rather not discuss it, either," she replied. "Come on, we've got to get out of this place."

Sabrina continued to carry Salem as they walked down the hall and right up to a fork in the road. One hallway led to the left while the other led to the right, and there was a door in the wall directly in front of her.

"Left, right, or center," Salem asked.

"Since we haven't come across any doors in this part of the maze, I think we should take it," Sabrina said, placing her hand on the knob.

"But maybe the door is closed for a reason," Salem warned her. "Remember what happened when you opened the door to the gingerbread house?"

"Salem, I think the door's here for a reason," she said. "I'm going to try it. If you want to continue down one of the halls, that's up to you."

"I think I liked you better when you weren't making decisions," Salem said. "Okay then. Let's go."

Sabrina turned the knob and walked through the doorway. It took them into another huge room like Candyworld, but there were no sugary treats or colored blocks in front of her. In fact, there was no path on the ground at all, just a ladder in the center of the room. Following the ladder with her eyes, Sabrina looked up to see a series of bridges suspended in the air. She also saw a bunch of ladders and slides connecting each of the levels of bridges with the ones above and below them.

"It looks like we're in Chutes and . . ." Then Sabrina saw the sign. "Slides and Climbing Devices?"

"The board game doesn't do it justice, does it?" Salem asked.

Sabrina's head craned in every direction. "This is the most amazing thing I've ever seen. Maybe this is an Amazing Maze!"

Paths upon paths crisscrossed overhead. Ladders stretched up at dizzying heights while slides twisted and sloped down and around. Hundreds of possible routes loomed above.

"Well, you'll have a lot of time to look at it," Salem said. "We have to work our way all the way up to that exit."

Sabrina's eyes followed up in the direction Salem's paw pointed. Near the ceiling of the huge room, off along the far back wall, Sabrina was able to see a tiny door.

"Well, what are we waiting for?" Sabrina asked as she started for the first ladder.

Salem whizzed past her. "Finally, a challenge!"

Together, they ascended the ladder, taking them up to the first bridge. Sabrina tentatively stepped off the ladder and determined that the walkway was sturdy and would support their weight.

She looked left and right and saw a ladder in each direction. The ladder to the left would take her up to the next bridge, but the ladder on the right would take her up to the bridge two levels above her. Looking down, she could see slides under some of the paths as well.

"So where do we go now?" Salem asked.

"I guess that ladder will take us higher," Sabrina said, pointing to the ladder on the right.

Together they moved in that direction. Sabrina carefully walked along the path since there weren't any railings to hold on to. They weren't too high from the ground, but Sabrina was still in no mood to fall. Salem on the other hand, was doing fine and had already reached the tall ladder.

"What's taking you so long?" he yelled back to Sabrina.

"I'm just trying to be careful," she called back.

"I didn't have any problems," Salem said.

Sabrina was closing in on him. "They're called *catwalks* for a reason, you know."

She finally reached the ladder and climbed

past two levels of paths, but they still had a while to go before they reached the exit by the ceiling.

Once on the new walkway, Sabrina surveyed the situation. Luckily the paths seemed to get wider as they got higher. Sabrina wasn't as nervous as she was on the lower path because she wasn't required to balance herself as much to walk.

Safely on the walkway, Sabrina saw even more ladders on the bridges surrounding them. The bad part about these wider paths was that it was now impossible to tell which of the blocks on the floor had slides under them.

Sabrina looked at the three paths that went out from the walkway they were on. "Since we took the middle door to start off this maze, maybe we should go with the middle path."

"Sounds good to me," Salem said.

Happy with herself for making the choice easily, Sabrina wasn't paying attention where she was walking until the floor dropped out from under her. Her rear hit the metal slide with a jarring bang as she quickly slid all the way back to the starting point.

When she finally came to a rest, she gave her sore bottom a little rub to ease the pain and looked up to see Salem far overhead laughing at her.

"That looked like fun!" he yelled from above. "I'm going to give it a try!"

"We don't have time for games!" Sabrina yelled back, getting up from the ground. "You just wait right there!"

"Spoilsport!" he yelled back.

Sabrina worked her way up the path she had just taken minutes ago. Even though she knew that it was a safe path, she was still careful about looking for slides. She was not about to make another stupid mistake.

She found Salem waiting for her at the top of the ladder. "Maybe I should choose the next path," he said.

"Go right ahead," she said as she pulled herself back up onto the bridge.

"Let's try left this time." He started down the path in that direction.

Sabrina stopped him before he got too far down the path. "Wait, let's check for slides first."

Sabrina bent down to the floor by the edge of the bridge and peered over the side. She saw no slides dropping out from under the path. Salem, being built closer to the ground, also leaned over and checked.

"Looks good from here," he said.

"I'd say so." Sabrina got back up on her feet. "Lead the way."

Once again Salem started down the path. Since they knew it was clear, they were able to walk quickly but carefully. When the bridge turned to the right, Salem did another quick check of the path and found it slide-free. Salem had apparently chosen the easiest path in the place. Although it took them on a winding route through the room, there were no side paths shooting out from it and, more important, no slides dropping out from under it. They continued along the easy path until it led them to a dead end. The path just ended in midair.

"No wonder we didn't have any problems." Sabrina looked over the edge of the walkway. "Now we have to go all the way back."

"Not necessarily," Salem said. "I think I see a way out."

Sabrina looked to her left and saw another hanging bridge about six feet away. This bridge had a ladder on it that would take them up three more levels of paths.

Sabrina immediately knew what he was suggesting. "You're crazy! I can't jump that."

"Sure you can," he said. "Just follow me."

Before Sabrina could utter another word of protest, Salem was gone. Using his natural cat abilities, he sailed over the gap between the bridges and landed on all fours, making up for his last botched landing when he fell on his face back in the Rat Trap room.

"See! It was easy!" he yelled from the other side.

Sabrina looked down over the edge of the bridge she was on. The drop was far enough to hurt her, but she could probably survive. Not exactly the confidence builder that she needed, but it would have to do. She took as many steps back as she could on the bridge. Pausing for a deep breath, she ran full out and jumped over the edge.

Miraculously she managed to land on the other side, on both her feet, letting out the breath of air she had been holding.

"Pretty good for a bi-ped," Salem said as he started up the ladder without giving Sabrina a moment to realize how crazy she was for doing what she just did.

Sabrina followed as the latest ladder took them up three levels. They were halfway to the top. When she was safely up, she noticed four paths to choose from shooting out in front of her.

"Should we go with the left path this time?" Salem asked.

"Wait! Look over there." Sabrina motioned to the path on the right.

"Where?" Salem looked in the direction she was pointing but only saw more paths, slides, and climbing devices.

"Over there," she insisted, practically throwing her arm out of joint to point.

On the opposite end of the room, on the same level they currently stood, Sabrina saw a huge ladder that stretched up the six levels to the top and would bring them directly to the exit. It appeared to be a shortcut through the upward maze. The only problem was that they would have to take several different paths to get all the way over to the bottom of the ladder.

"Let's go!" As soon as he saw what she was pointing at, Salem took off toward the ladder.

"Salem, slow down!" Sabrina yelled, trying to keep up.

But the excitement of the discovery had overcome Salem, and he paid no heed to her calls. For the moment he had forgotten all about the slides as he turned the first corner of one of the intersecting paths. He was suddenly reminded of the pitfalls when he no longer felt that there was a floor beneath him.

Realizing that Salem had unwittingly made sure that the path was clear for her, Sabrina was able to increase her speed and catch up to him. When she saw the floor fall out from under him, she dropped to the ground, sliding forward on her stomach right up to the edge of the path. In a spectacular move she managed to grab Salem's tail and stop him from falling down the slide.

Salem dangled from her grasp, swinging from left to right. "Well, this is embarrassing."

"You've put on weight," Sabrina said as she pulled him up. "Must have been all the candy you ate."

"You know, I never point out when you've put on a few pounds," Salem said.

Sabrina lifted him into her arms so that he wouldn't take off again. "You can complain when you start carrying me around."

She took a few steps back. Then, with Salem still firmly in her arms, she jumped across the opening in the walkway. Safely on the other side, she continued along the path. She put Salem down and told him to follow her.

Several more pathways brought them closer to the long ladder until there were only a few squares between them and the final "climbing device" that would move them on to the next part of the maze. The only problem was that Sabrina could see that a slide was under one of the squares, but she couldn't see which one it was under.

Carefully she slid her left foot forward, putting her weight down onto the square. When the square didn't budge, she slid her right foot forward. With both feet in the square, Sabrina waited to see if it would fall.

Nothing happened.

Only three more squares to go. Since the third square had the ladder on it, she figured that the slide had to be under one of the next two blocks. Again, she repeated her left-foot, right-foot slide. She stood firmly on the square, looking warily at the next.

"I guess the slide is under this one," Sabrina said.

Again, she took a few steps back before running and jumping over the square. She easily cleared it, landing right next to the ladder.

When Salem saw that she was safe, he followed suit and scurried up the ladder with ease. Sabrina had a bit of a harder time because the long climb was tiring, especially since she had been carrying extra weight in the form of Salem for much of the maze.

Finally they found themselves next to the exit door, with no apparent traps in the way. Breathing heavily from the climb, Sabrina went to open the door. As soon as her hand touched the knob, it turned on its own and the door swung open. On the other side of the door stood Skippy, the assistant to Drell, the head of the Witches' Council.

Sabrina had not seen Skippy for years. In fact, she hadn't seen Drell for years, either, but she didn't really mind that and neither did her aunt Hilda, who had a rocky relationship with the head of the Witches' Council. Drell was the witch who punished Salem by turning him into a cat and also made Sabrina's life miserable the year she found out she was a witch.

Although Skippy never said a word to her, he was always kind and helpful, especially when Drell was being his meanest. The little man was dressed in an old-fashioned black suit with wide lapels and a round hat covering much of his curly brown hair. He was also wearing the same cute smile he always wore.

"Skippy, what are you doing here?" Sabrina asked, momentarily forgetting that Skippy never spoke.

He made a series of hand gestures followed by some crazy body movements. All in all, it looked as if he was trying to relate a story to Sabrina, but she had no idea what he was saying.

Sabrina remembered that Skippy had helped her find her friend Jenny when she got lost in the Other Realm, and now she hoped that he could guide her out of the maze. "Are you here to help me . . . or are you stuck here, too?"

Skippy nodded his head "yes," but Sabrina didn't know which question he was answering.

Sabrina started to ask for a clarification. "But which—"

Before she could finish, Skippy turned and skipped away from her.

"I guess we know why he's called Skippy," Salem said.

Sabrina was already moving after him. "Come on, Salem. He may know a way out."

Chapter 10

Sabrina and Salem followed as Skippy rounded a corner. They came across yet another multicolored hallway.

This time there were six rows of colored squares on the floor. Each row had a red square, a blue square, a green square, and a yellow square. The colors seemed to be in a random order in each row.

Skippy hadn't started across the squares yet. He was waiting for Sabrina and Salem to reach him. Once they caught up, and he was sure they were paying attention, Skippy took off his little round hat and threw it over the colored rows. As soon as it crossed over the first green square, it disappeared. He pointed at the green square, then he pointed at Sabrina and Salem with a little wag of his finger that Sabrina knew to be the universal sign for "no."

"So, we shouldn't step on the green squares?" Sabrina asked.

Skippy shook his head "no." He pointed to himself and then turned to the rows of colors. With an overly exaggerated step, he put his left foot down on a red square. After looking back to make sure that Sabrina and Salem were watching carefully, Skippy moved his right foot onto the square and made a "ta-da"-like gesture.

"I think he means we should follow him," Sabrina said to Salem.

"I can't believe this is our fearless leader," Salem said.

Skippy shot the cat a dark look.

Knowing he would not apologize for his own rudeness, Sabrina did it for him. "I'm sorry, Skippy, he's just . . . well . . . he's Salem."

Skippy nodded his acceptance of her apology as if her explanation seemed to say it all. Then he moved to the red square on the next row, smiling as he went.

"Come on," Sabrina said as she stepped onto the first red square. "We'd better do as Skippy says."

Salem reluctantly followed.

After Skippy moved off the second red square, he moved to a green one.

"This is kind of fun," Sabrina said. "A lot like hopscotch."

"Woo-hoo," Salem groaned, to indicate how much fun he was *not* having.

This time both Skippy *and* Sabrina shot him a dirty look.

Sabrina and Salem followed Skippy as he moved onto a blue square, then another blue. Once they caught up with him, Skippy turned to them and gave a little bow and a wave.

"Hey, we're not there yet," Salem protested.

Skippy's smile grew wider than Sabrina had ever seen it before. Sweetly he blew her a little kiss before leaning over to the red square that was right next to the safe blue square he was standing on.

"Skippy, wait!" Sabrina yelled.

But it was too late. Skippy fell onto the red square and disappeared, leaving Sabrina and Salem with one more row of squares to cross on their own.

"I knew we couldn't trust him," Salem said. "Any friend of Drell's—"

Sabrina cut him off. "If you had been a little nicer to him, maybe he wouldn't have abandoned us. Now what do we do?"

Sabrina looked at the final row of colored squares. One of the squares would safely take her to the rest of the maze, while the other squares would take her somewhere she probably didn't want to go.

"Okay, think," she said. Turning, she looked back to the colored rows she had just crossed over. She reworked the path in her head.

"Should we flip a coin?" Salem asked.

Sabrina was getting a little annoyed with his

negative attitude. "You know, Salem, if you don't have anything positive to say, you can just step on that little red square and get out of here. I've gotten this far and I think I can figure this out."

"I only meant—"

"Salem, shush." Sabrina stopped him since she almost had the solution worked out. "I think there's a pattern to the route. The first squares we walked on were red, red, and green. Then we stepped on a blue and another blue. That means the last square we have to step on is this yellow one. So the pattern is red, red, green, blue, blue, yellow!" She pointed to the square in front of her.

"I hope you're right," Salem said in a threatening tone. Not that he would do anything to her if she was wrong, but he always used that tone to make himself seem more menacing than he actually was.

"I am," she said, and she was certain of that fact. Without even a moment of hesitation, Sabrina stepped onto the yellow square.

Nothing happened.

"I knew it all along," Salem said as he followed onto the square.

Together they stepped off the final row and back onto the bland white hallway. Looking back on what she had just done on her own, Sabrina gave herself a mental pat on the back then realized just how exhausting the Amazing Maze had been so far.

"Let's rest for a minute," Sabrina said as she

sat down on the floor. "This is all getting to be a little too much for me."

As soon as Salem joined her on the ground, they heard something very large and very loud coming their way.

"That doesn't sound good," the cat said, back up on all four feet.

Without waiting to find out what was coming, Sabrina was up as well as they took off in the opposite direction. Figuring the best way to outrun it would be to outwit it, Sabrina began turning corners—left, right, and left again—without bothering to worry about where she was heading. Salem's flight instinct had also taken over, and he followed without question.

Turning one last corner, they wound up in another long hallway with no alternate routes ahead of them. Moving at top speed, they ran for what seemed like blocks before finally stopping at an intersection. Sabrina listened for a moment, straining to hear over her own heavy breathing.

The loud noise was off in the distance.

"Do you think we're safe?" she asked Salem.

His wide eyes told her that he didn't think so.

Catching one deep breath of air, Sabrina looked back down the long hallway to see a massive silver metal ball had just turned the corner and was rolling toward them. The ball filled the entire hallway, and the sound it made grew louder as it got closer to them.

Sabrina and Salem took off down the hall on

their right. Immediately realizing that they had chosen the wrong route as they came across a hole in the floor.

Stopping short, Sabrina looked down the hole, hoping for a means of escape. All she could see was darkness. All she could hear was the giant silver ball getting closer. Sabrina and Salem quickly jumped across the hole and continued.

No matter how they twisted and turned through the maze, the ball continued to follow and more holes continued to pop up in the road. Sabrina could tell that the holes were growing larger since she and Salem had to jump farther and farther the longer they ran.

"Don't say it," Salem warned her.

"Say what?" she asked, panting heavily from the exhaustion.

"What people usually say in these situations," he replied.

"What?" she asked again, then realized what he meant. "I learned long ago never to say a magical situation can't get any worse."

And, even though Sabrina had already learned that lesson, the situation did, indeed, get worse.

Sabrina and Salem were flung against the wall as the floor rose up and the entire maze suddenly shifted to the left.

"But I didn't say it!" Sabrina pleaded, hoping Quizmaster or whoever controlled the maze was listening to her.

Whether anyone was listening or not no longer

mattered since the maze responded by violently shifting to the right.

Sabrina and Salem continued their wobbly run through the maze with the giant silver ball getting ever closer and the holes in the ground growing ever larger and the maze shifting ever harder, left, right, back, and forth. They ran and jumped until they came across the biggest hole they had ever seen.

"Wow, that's the biggest hole I've ever seen," Salem said.

Since they had seen it long before they reached it, Sabrina and Salem had plenty of time to stop running before they fell into the hole. Peering over the edge they had hoped that this hole would provide them with an escape route, but they still could not see the bottom. Due to the last turns they had taken, they had put enough distance between themselves and the ball so that, once again, it could be heard but not seen. But they knew that it was still coming.

Sabrina pulled Salem back as the maze lurched forward.

"We can't jump that," she said. "It's twice the size of the jump we had to do back in the chutes . . . I mean . . . Slides and Climbing Devices."

"Well, we can't wait here and we can't go back. I'd say we're out of options," Salem reminded her as they lurched to the left.

"If only I had my magic," Sabrina said.

"How did you get out of situations like this before you knew you were a witch?" Salem asked as they lurched to the right.

"I was never *in* situations like this before I knew I was a witch!" she yelled as the maze sprang backward.

"Oh, sorry," Salem sheepishly said. "Being born a full witch, I tend to forget that the Mortal Realm isn't always as interesting as this one."

The sound of the rolling ball cut their conversation short as they bounced forward again, nearly tipping into the hole.

"Wait a minute," Sabrina said, thinking back to the other problems they had faced so far in the now aptly named Amazing Maze.

"We don't have a minute," Salem reminded her as they fell against the left wall of the maze.

"Have you noticed that there's a pattern to the motion of the maze?" Sabrina asked.

A shift to the right landed Salem on his rear. "You and your patterns. Yeah, the pattern is, the maze moves, we fall down."

"No, it seems to be moving left then right, then backward and forward," she said, struggling to stay on her feet.

"And what good is that information going to do us?" Salem asked as they fell back.

They could see the giant silver ball making the last turn. Somehow it seemed to be larger than the last time they saw it. It also seemed to be rolling much faster. It would be on them in seconds.

"No time to explain." Sabrina scooped Salem up in her arms and began to run toward the ball.

"Wrong way! Wrong way!" Salem yelled.

As the ball got closer, Sabrina turned back to the hole.

"Wrong way! Wrong way!" he yelled again.

"Quiet!" Sabrina said as she held him tighter. "I hope this works."

As Sabrina reached the edge of the hole, the entire maze lurched forward again. Using the force of the maze like a springboard, Sabrina jumped across the hole. The momentum from the lurch, combined with Sabrina's jump, sent them sailing to the other side.

Sabrina threw Salem from her arms as she landed in a roll, coming to a stop curled up on the ground.

Rubbing her now sore ankles, Sabrina stayed on the ground and turned to watch as the giant ball fell into the even bigger hole.

Safe at last.

"That's our girl," Aunt Zelda said behind her.

"Aunt Zelda! Aunt Hilda!" Sabrina got up from the ground to go hug her aunts, who had magically appeared. Her ankles felt okay when she put weight on them, but she still stopped herself before she reached her aunts. "You're probably holograms, aren't you?"

"And what kind of riddle do you have for us?" Salem asked as he righted himself. "Something else pointless and inane I suspect."

"Salem, don't talk like that!" Sabrina said.

"Sabrina, they're holograms," Salem reminded her of what she had just said. "We can say whatever we want to them, like telling Zelda that her egghead class lectures are really boring or that Hilda's coffee tastes like gasoline."

Zelda and Hilda stood where they were, not responding to the insults. Neither Sabrina nor Salem noticed that their hands had balled into fists.

"Try it," Salem prodded her, "it's fun!"

"Yes, Sabrina," Zelda said through clenched teeth.

"Try it," Hilda added.

Sabrina looked at the duplicate aunts and remembered back to Harvey. She figured that if he had been real, her aunts might be real, too. She considered warning Salem, but he had been so annoying throughout much of this ordeal that she left him on his own. "We're on a bit of a schedule, so if you could just ask us your riddle, we'd like to get moving."

"We don't have a riddle for you," Hilda said.

"We just have one little question," Zelda added.

"You know, we just met some rats that remind me a little of you guys," Salem said. "How 'bout we try this without finishing each other's sentences?"

"You're really enjoying this, aren't you?" Sabrina asked him.

Salem just smiled and nodded vigorously.

"I know you're just holograms," Sabrina said

to her possibly fake aunts. "But I apologize for him . . . again!"

"No apology necessary," Hilda said. "He'll get his eventually."

Salem silently shuddered at the threat, not knowing what the maze had in store for him.

"But as you said, you do have a time limit, so we should be moving along," Zelda chimed in.

"The question?" Sabrina asked.

"It's simple really," Zelda said. "Do you think you can manage the rest of the maze on your own, without Salem?"

That question caught her off guard. She hadn't even wondered what it would have been like if she didn't have Salem to help her along through the maze. The only time they were separated was when she was with Harvey, and the Quizmaster was there to keep her company. She hadn't been alone since she entered the maze. Sure, Salem may not have been the most helpful partner, and tended to be downright annoying at times, but Sabrina didn't know if she could do it alone. She didn't know if she *wanted* to do it alone.

"How much longer do I have to go?" she asked.

"It would be cheating to tell you," Hilda said. "But—"

Zelda quickly jumped in. "How long depends on how you traverse the next part of the maze. But we do warn you that the hardest part is yet to come."

"What if I say that I still need Salem?" Sabrina said.

"You could have said that like you really meant it," Salem said.

"I do," Sabrina replied. "You *have* been helpful at times."

"And my reward is being trapped in this maze with you? Gee, thanks."

"Then again, maybe he has been around too long," Sabrina said. "What would happen to him if I let him go?"

"Oh, we'll take care of him," Hilda said ominously.

Sabrina kind of liked the way she said that. Salem, on the other hand, did not like the response one bit.

"I guess I can do it alone," Sabrina said. "I was pretty good at getting away from that gigantic ball that was chasing us down."

"A good example of thinking on your feet," Zelda said.

"Or on the run, is more like it," Hilda said. "We do finish each other's sentences too much, don't we?"

"Never mind," Zelda said. "Sabrina, have you made your decision?"

Sabrina looked at Salem, then back at her aunts. "I think I can do this."

"Wonderful," Zelda said as she and Hilda moved out of Sabrina's way.

"There you go, kiddo," Hilda said as she

motioned to the path before them. "Good luck."

"Thanks," Sabrina said as she started back down the maze.

As soon as Sabrina turned a corner and was out of earshot, Zelda picked Salem up off the ground.

"Now, as for you," she said to the cat in a menacing tone.

"Like I'm afraid of a couple of holograms." He laughed in response to what he believed to be an empty threat.

"Holograms?" Hilda asked. "Who said we were holograms?"

"Certainly not this egghead lecturer," Zelda answered.

"You are so busted," Hilda added. All Salem could say was, "Geh?!"

Two turns down the maze, Sabrina couldn't hear Salem's cries for help. Instead, being alone for the first time in hours, she started talking to herself, in place of a real traveling companion.

"I can do this," she said. "I did escape the ball, and Salem really wasn't much more than someone to bounce ideas off. In fact, except for a few turns, he really wasn't that much of a help at all. And this maze isn't all that bad. What could it possibly throw at me that I can't handle?"

Suddenly a balled-up piece of paper flew at her, smacking her in the face.

"Do you always have to be so literal?" Sabrina yelled out to the maze.

Sabrina bent to pick up the trash that had bounced off her face and fallen to the floor. Unwrapping the paper, she was surprised to find that it was one of her attempts at scheduling. In fact, it was her final choice of schedule. The one that she had lived thanks to the Magic Cue Ball.

"What am I supposed to do with this?" she asked the maze.

The maze responded when a door suddenly appeared next to Sabrina.

"Thank you," she said to the maze.

Figuring that the maze was trying to help her, Sabrina walked through the door without a second thought. She hoped that this was a sign that she was near the end.

Once through the door, Sabrina found herself in one of her college classrooms. For a moment, she thought she had been sent home, but when she looked at the walls she knew the room wasn't real.

Instead of a blackboard, charts, or pictures, the walls were covered with little white rectangles. When Sabrina moved closer to them, she noticed that each rectangle had words on it like *American Literature* or *Sociology.* She pulled a white rectangle off the wall—it read *Psychology*—and noticed that it was actually a magnet. The room reminded her one of those refrigerator magnet poem kits where she would take different words and make a poem on her kitchen appliance. Only this one was industrial-sized.

"Okay, maze," Sabrina said. "You brought me here. Now what do I do?"

"Attention class! Attention class!" Quizmaster said from the front of the room.

When Sabrina turned, she saw him standing behind the professor's desk. He was dressed in a gray suit jacket and dark jeans, just like Professor Murphy wore.

"What happened to you?" Sabrina asked, referring to his clothes. This was the first normal outfit she had ever seen him wear.

"You like it?" he asked, modeling the new threads. "I'm trying something new."

"I don't know," Sabrina said. "I'm more used to you in colors."

"Well, that is what I'm known for." Quizmaster came out from behind the desk and lifted his pant leg to show Sabrina that he still wore bright socks.

"Much better," she said before getting to the issue at hand. "So what are we doing here, and are you bringing any other old boyfriends I don't want to see?"

"No, this is just you alone," he said as he walked her to the center of the room. "Do you think you can handle it?"

"I guess," Sabrina said. "But what's with the room?"

Quizmaster stopped and motioned to the white rectangles on the walls. "These are all the classes you were deciding from when you were making your schedule."

"I thought some of them looked familiar," Sabrina said. "But why are they here? I already know what classes I'm taking."

"You might want to sit down for this," Quizmaster said as he motioned to a seat beside him.

Sabrina chose to remain standing. "I don't think I'm going to like this."

"While you were in the maze," he said, "the scheduling office closed for the week. The classes you chose with the help of the Cue Ball are all full."

"All of them?" she asked in a high-pitched voice, showing her surprise. "Every single class is closed?"

"Well, except your aunt's physics class," he said. "Which is why you're here. You have to choose a new schedule before you can leave the maze."

Sabrina looked around the room, horrified. "You mean, from all these choices?"

There were literally hundreds of magnetic rectangles around the room and Sabrina knew them all by heart. She had gone through so many different schedules trying to come up with the perfect one.

"You have five minutes," Quizmaster said, and the grandfather clock appeared beside him showing that what he said was true.

"Five minutes!" She was terrified. It had taken forever to choose a schedule the first time she did it. Sabrina didn't know if she could do it now without magical aid or anyone to help her. But she did know that if she couldn't settle on a schedule, she would be trapped in the maze forever.

Quizmaster went back to the front of the room and produced an easel out of thin air. "Place your final choices here."

Sabrina followed him to the front. "But I can't do this."

He just ignored her as he sat behind the desk, picking up a newspaper to read. Quizmaster looked to the clock and saw that the second hand was approaching twelve. "The test begins . . . now."

Sabrina ran to the nearest wall and began reading the class choices. There were so many.

"How am I supposed to go through all these classes in five minutes?" she asked.

Quizmaster didn't even look up from his paper. "No talking during the test."

"Thanks for the help," she mumbled to herself.

Sabrina returned her attention to the wall. She could feel the seconds ticking away behind her. She picked up a magnetic rectangle that read *Spanish*. Remembering what Miles had said, she moved to the easel and was about to put it on her schedule.

"Why am I doing this?" she asked herself. "I already took some Spanish in high school. I want to learn something else."

Quizmaster stayed focused on his paper.

"But Miles did say that I shouldn't take French,"

Sabrina continued to herself. "But why am I so worried about what Miles thinks? Why am I so worried about what everyone else thinks? This is my schedule. This is my life. Why do I keep asking other people to tell me what to do?"

Sabrina put the Spanish rectangle back where it came from and approached Quizmaster. "Is that what this is all about? I keep waiting for people to tell me what to do or how they're going to react. Is that why I can't make any decisions?"

Sabrina waited for Quizmaster to say something. He just turned a page on his paper.

"I'm doing it again," she said, turning away from him. "I only started really moving through this maze when I stopped worrying about Salem, or my holographic friends, or Harvey, and started making decisions based on what *I* wanted." She scanned the room with her eyes. "And I want to take French."

As soon as the words were out of her mouth, a rectangle across the room began to glow brightly. Sabrina ran to it and, seeing that it said *French*, took it to the front of the room and placed it on her schedule.

She didn't notice the smile Quizmaster had on his face as he pretended to read the paper.

Sabrina turned back into the room, stopping to think. "Okay, what other classes did I want to take?" She thought about her many schedules, remembering the two journalism classes she had chosen the day before: *British Journalism* and

Propaganda Through the Ages. Roxie had told her not to take them, but Sabrina thought they sounded interesting. Since this was her schedule she was working on, Sabrina turned and scanned the room until their two rectangles lit up. She ran to the spots, retrieved them, and put them on the schedule board. Things were starting to look up.

"Now I should take some fun classes." She remembered that her class adviser had warned her about doing this. He seemed to think school was only for hard work, but Sabrina totally believed in those public service announcements that said learning can be fun. This time she didn't even have to think of the classes before they lit up. Sabrina ran through the room and back, placing *Intro to Theater* and *Fencing* on the board.

She looked at the one remaining empty space on her schedule and looked at the grandfather clock that showed less than a minute. "I guess I should take a science."

Sabrina didn't notice that Quizmaster was not only smiling, but he was nodding his head slightly as well.

"I guess I'll take Aunt Zelda's," she said.

"Are you sure?" Quizmaster asked without looking up.

"Oh, look who's talking now?" she said. "Yes, I'm sure. I am interested in the subject, and I would like to have her as a teacher at least once."

Finally Quizmaster looked directly at her. "Well, don't let me stop you."

The two smiled at each other, and Sabrina ran to the glowing rectangle and put it on her schedule. The entire schedule beamed brightly.

"Good job!" Quizmaster said before he, the grandfather clock, and everything else around Sabrina disappeared.

Chapter 11

Once Sabrina made her final decision, she had expected to be brought back to the maze, so she was surprised when she wound up in her college bedroom. Wondering if this was another test, she checked the room for anything out of the ordinary. Everything seemed fine except for the remains of the Magic Cue Ball that had exploded on her floor, leaving a burn mark on the rug.

"I'm going to have to get that cleaned before Roxie sees it," she said, rubbing at the mark and picking up the shards of cue ball. Remembering that she was free of the maze, Sabrina gave a little point of her finger and the scorch mark disappeared while the cue ball returned to its normal, nonmagical self. Since the cue ball was no longer glowing, Sabrina figured it was safe to send it back to its rightful place on the pool table in the Student Union.

Otherwise, the room looked fine, except for the mess of balled-up papers that still littered the floor. Figuring there was no time like the present, Sabrina threw all the paper into the trash, since she finally had her schedule done and ready to go for next Monday when the scheduling office opened again.

It wasn't until Sabrina realized she was exhausted and went to lie on her bed that she noticed the odd pink pillow she had never seen before. Knowing that Roxie didn't own anything that was pink, Sabrina carefully touched the fake fur pillow expecting some kind of magical trap. As she lifted the pillow, it unexpectedly uncurled.

"Please don't say anything," Salem, his fur a bright shade of pink, whined as he was lifted from the bed. "Leave me some dignity."

Sabrina tried as hard as she could not to laugh. She failed.

"What happened to you?" Sabrina asked once she regained her composure.

Salem couldn't look at her directly. "You know those two holograms of your aunts we ran into in the maze?"

"Yes."

"Well, they weren't," he said.

"They weren't my aunts?" Sabrina didn't quite get what he was saying.

"They weren't holograms," he said.

Suddenly everything became clear to Sabrina, and she started laughing again. "It's not like you didn't deserve it. You did say some pretty nasty things."

"I didn't come here to be made fun of," Salem whined. "I had enough of that from the alley cats I ran into on the way over. I came here to be alone, wallowing in my misery."

Sabrina put him back down on her bed. "Sorry, Salem, but I'm going be here all night."

"What about the sorority party?" he asked, curling back up to look like a pillow again. "And getting a new dress?"

"I'm not joining the sorority. Even though Morgan really wants me to, it's just too much work. Since I'm not joining, I can miss this party." Sabrina sat at her desk and turned on her computer. "I've got homework to do anyway."

The door to Sabrina's room opened, and Salem tucked his head into his body so he could complete his pillow impression. Sabrina laughed at the cat's attempt at hiding as Roxie came into the room.

"You can't believe the day I just had," Roxie said, dropping her books on her own bed before she realized that Sabrina wasn't supposed to be there. "Wait. Weren't you supposed to be at that stupid sorority mixer?"

"Changed my mind," Sabrina said.

"Good. You have enough work to do with me on the newspaper. You don't have the time to be spending it all with a bunch of giggling sorority girls." Roxie turned on her own computer so she could check her e-mail. "You'll notice that I haven't brought up the tennis lessons."

Sabrina suddenly remembered that she had forgotten all about her friend's request. "Yes. Tennis lessons. I think they would be fun. Count me in."

"Really?" Roxie did not sound as excited as Sabrina did, but that was Roxie. "You're going to do it?"

"Yes," Sabrina repeated herself. "I've made my decision."

"Thanks," Roxie said.

"If you'll excuse me," Sabrina said, getting up from her chair, "I have a call to make."

"Whatever," Roxie said in her usual noncommittal tone.

As Sabrina went for the bedroom door, she stopped herself, unable to resist. "Oh, and if Salem bothers you while I'm on the phone, you can put him out of the room."

Sabrina heard him moan from inside his curled-up little ball.

"Your cat's here?" Roxie said, looking around the room for his black fur. "Where is he?"

Sabrina pointed to the pink powder puff on her bed. "Right there. My aunts were experimenting with hair dye."

Roxie looked at the oddly colored cat. "You're aunts need to get more interesting lives." Then she got up to examine him a little closer. "Although he does look cute in a bizarre sort of way."

As Sabrina left the room, she heard Salem grunt an angry "Meow!"

Smiling, Sabrina walked to the kitchen to grab the phone. On her way she stopped when she saw Miles lying on the couch with his eyes open, staring at the ceiling.

"Miles, what are you doing?" she asked standing over him.

"Trying to teach myself to sleep with my eyes open," he explained as if it were the most normal thing in the world to do. "That way I'll be ready if the aliens try to come and get me at night."

"Okay." Sabrina was used to his crazy ideas by now. "But you had some favor you wanted to ask me?"

Miles perked up when she reminded him about what she had cut him off on earlier in the day. "Yeah, I heard there was a position open in the school science department as your aunt's assistant. I was wondering if you knew if she had filled it."

"Actually, she hasn't yet, but I can put a good word in for you," Conveniently, Sabrina was already on her way to call her aunt about that very subject.

"Could you?" Miles was nearly beside himself with excitement. "That would be great."

Sabrina smiled, considering the joy he got from what she expected to be a rather boring job. "I couldn't think of a better assistant."

"Thanks, Sabrina," he said as he ran to his room.

Sabrina continued over to the phone and dialed her aunts' number.

"Hello, Sabrina," Hilda said as she picked up the phone.

"Did you get caller ID?" Sabrina asked since Hilda knew who was on the line before she had even spoken.

"No, Sabrina. I'm a witch," Hilda reminded her. "I've had magical caller ID since phones were invented. Are you feeling better? I didn't mean to overload you with questions."

"Much better," Sabrina said. "And that's kind of why I called. I'd be glad to pick up extra shifts at the coffeehouse until you have someone for the late shift."

"Are you sure?" Hilda asked, still concerned for her niece. "Because I can just have Josh—"

"I'm sure," Sabrina said, hoping that she could give poor Josh a break from Hilda's crazy workload. Besides, she could use the extra cash. "And can you tell Aunt Zelda that I won't be able to be her assistant, but I have the perfect candidate for her?"

"Sure," Hilda said. "Is that all, because I have to get going. Drell called out of the blue, and we have a date tonight."

Sabrina was not exactly thrilled to hear about her aunt's plans with Drell, but she didn't let on. "Yeah, that's all. Oh, I did want to say that I loved what you and Aunt Zelda did to Salem."

"Wasn't that great?" Hilda got another laugh

from her own mischief. "Wait about two more hours. He's going to turn bright purple."

Sabrina joined in on the laughter. "I'll be sure to coordinate my P.J.s to match."

"Talk to you later, Sabrina," Hilda said from her end of the line.

"All right. Bye," Sabrina said, and she hung up wondering if she should tell Salem about his destined change of color. As she walked to her room, she decided to let him find out on his own.

When Sabrina got back to the room, she found Roxie carrying Salem and looking as if she was about to go somewhere with him.

"Do you mind if I take Salem out for a little bit?" Roxie asked. "I have a professor who I'm trying to score some extra points with. She has a house full of cats and I know if I bring Salem over like this to see her, I'll score major brownie points."

"Sure. I just need him back in about two hours." Sabrina couldn't resist the thought of Pink Salem being seen by a house full of cats, although she knew it would be best to get him back before he magically changed to purple.

"Thanks." Roxie started for the door.

"Before you go." Sabrina stopped her. "Would you consider getting a position in student government to be in conflict with the kind of investigative reporting we're trying to do for the school paper?"

Roxie gave her a look. "Duh."

"I thought so, too," Sabrina said. "Have fun with the cats."

Even though Sabrina already had decided not to join student government, it was nice to have someone back up her decision. It was an even better feeling to know that she had made the decision on her own without waiting for Roxie to tell her what to do.

Sabrina could hear Salem's protesting meows long after Roxie had left the house.

Sabrina sat back at her computer trying to get some homework out of the way even though it was a Friday night. She started to list possible subjects for her history report, but nothing really stood out.

Then, by fate, or maybe Quizmaster's doing, a picture fell off her wall. Rather than getting up to put it back, Sabrina was struck by a sudden idea. She knew the perfect subject for her report: A woman who knew all about the direction she had wanted to go in and never doubted her decisions even when the world may have told her she was crazy. Sabrina went on-line to find out everything she could about Amelia Earhart.

About the Author

Paul Ruditis used to work in Hollywood, where he was surrounded by people who seemed to be from other planets. His first published short story, "The Show Must Go On," is part of the *Buffy, The Vampire Slayer* collection, *How I Survived My Summer Vacation*. Paul has also written *Roswell Pop Quiz*.